THE CROOKED SHERIFF

Black Pete Bowen quit Texas with a burning hatred of men who try to take the law into their own hands. But he discovers that things aren't much different in the silver mountains of Arizona. A young psychopath has elected himself sheriff and is intent on running a Mexican rancher and his daughter off their land. With his twin guns blazing, young Black Pete brings the confrontation to an explosive end.

JOHN DYSON

THE CROOKED SHERIFF

Complete and Unabridged

LINFORD
Leicester

First published in Great Britain in 1995 by
Robert Hale Limited
London

First Linford Edition
published 1997
by arrangement with
Robert Hale Limited
London

The right of John Dyson to be identified as
the author of this work has been asserted by him
in accordance with the
Copyright, Designs and Patents Act, 1988

British Library CIP Data

Dyson, John, *1943–*
    The crooked sheriff.—Large print ed.—
Linford western library
    1. English fiction—20th century
    2. Large type books
    I. Title
    823.9′14 [F]

    ISBN 0–7089–7986–6

Published by
F. A. Thorpe (Publishing) Ltd.
Anstey, Leicestershire

Set by Words & Graphics Ltd.
Anstey, Leicestershire
Printed and bound in Great Britain by
T. J. Press (Padstow) Ltd., Padstow, Cornwall

This book is printed on acid-free paper

To Jean,
Black Pete's
No. 1 fan.

1

THE lone rider came out of the hills on his grey filly, forded the Pecos, and reined in when he saw the collection of ramshackle timber dwellings which served as a town. Langtry, the sign said. Something warned him to keep going, bypass it, get over the state border to safety. But he had been travelling a long time. The horse had carried him across the plains of Texas as far as this desolate north-west corner. She deserved a night in a livery, a morral of split corn.

The rider was shabbily dressed, a tattered mackinaw over a canvas shirt, tight leather leggings on his long legs and boots bursting at the seams. A thick red bandanna was wrapped high around his throat and a low-crowned black hat shielded his eyes from the fierce sun. He licked his parched lips

1

at the prospect of a shot of whiskey, a hot bath, some human communication. A man could sure get tired of talking to his horse. He nudged the filly forward: "Geddit, hoss."

The town was deathly quiet as he walked the horse into the dusty main street, but he had the sensation of eyes watching him. A few scrubby cow-ponies were hitched to a rail, sullen and beat-looking in the afternoon heat, motionless apart from the flick of a tail, or a kick as they were pestered by flies. Two old biddys in poke bonnets and long dresses stood gossiping with their baskets outside a general store. They turned to watch the dark-bearded stranger as his horse ambled by. They noted the Winchester rifle, jutting from the saddle-boot, the brace of revolvers hung handles forward on his ammunition belt. He might have been a Texas Ranger after a fugitive. Or a fugitive himself.

The clang of metal on anvil drew the rider towards a tumbledown livery.

Pete Bowen, for that was his name, stepped down, and wiped the sweat from his forehead. He was a man in his mid-twenties, wide-shouldered, a thick mass of crow-black hair badly in need of a cut hanging down over his collar. Maybe that was why they called him Black Pete. Or maybe it was the melancholy set of his hardcut features. He had not much to be cheerful about. Three weeks before he had been a rancher with money in the bank. Now, his house burned, his wife killed, his young son sent to live with an aunt, he was a hunted murderer with a price on his head.

"What can I do for you?" the smith asked.

"A night's livery for my hoss."

"Two dollars in advance. Where you headin'?"

"I ain't sure."

"Or ain't saying?" The smith gave a hollow laugh as he pocketed the silver and eyed the stranger. "Well, whichever direction, there sure is some harsh thirsty country out there. Man needs a good horse. And this is a feisty beast you have here."

"She ain't a beast. She's damn near human. Raised her myself from a foal. See she gets the best. OK?"

"Sure. She'll be over in the far stall."

"Have her saddled for me in the morning. This town got a saloon?"

"Down the road a piece on the edge of town. You can't miss it. Under the hanging-tree. Owned by Judge Roy Bean. You better watch out for him. He's some ornery character."

"That so? Aincha got no lawman?"

"Like the judge says, he's the only law west of the Pecos."

"Yep. I think I've heard of him."

Pete uncinched the filly's saddle, with his rifle, saddle-bags and blanket-roll, and dumped them in the stall. He gave her a friendly slap over the quarters, and went to take a look at the town. First stop was an eatery to fill his stomach with beans and *frijoles*. There was a billiards-hall and bath-house next door.

4

He paid a dollar and soaked himself in a soapy tub, washed away the dirt of travel. That was better. Made him feel like a new man. He buttoned his double-breasted blue shirt, pulled his shotgun chaps over his worn jeans, and tied the bandanna tight around, to hide the raw throatburn from the hanging. He hitched his gunbelt over his hips, loosened the revolvers in his holsters and stepped out into the sunlight.

The saloon was a low-slung timbered building with a shingled roof, plastered with crudely-painted signs: 'The Jersey Lilly' (the painter could have done with a dictionary); 'Judge Roy Bean, proprietor, noterry public, justice of piece'. But the one which interested Pete was 'Ice beer'.

He paused as he pushed through the swing doors, his eyes unaccustomed to the gloom, but there appeared to be just a few *hombres* in dusty clothes and sombreros leaned on the bar or sprawled at crude tables and chairs along the walls. Torn and fading theatre posters from far-off cities were plastered above the bar, all of them advertising the appearance of Lily Langtry at one time or another. And an oil-painting purporting to be the damsel herself took pride of place.

All conversation ceased as Black Pete strode across to the bar, his spurs rattling on the wooden floorboards. The men watched him curiously.

His voice was still hoarse and husky from the hanging. "Gimme one of them ice beers," he said to the Mexican boy tending the bar. "And a bottle of whiskey."

He slapped a double eagle down, pulled the cork of the bottle with his teeth, spat it away to show he meant business, tipped the raw whiskey to his lips and took a long pull. He picked up the glass of beer and sank it in one as a chaser. It wasn't exactly iced, but it was cold and it was delicious.

Pete pushed it forward for a refill and croaked out, "Somebody here a fan of this lady?"

An old whitebeard in a straw hat chuckled. "That's the judge. He's crazy about her. You be careful what you say about that gal, son."

"An English actress, ain't she? Hobnobs with royalty. He even met her?"

"Nope. But he sure aims to. He's sent her a special invitation to this town he's named after her."

A thin, crooked-face man with greased-back hair gave a guffaw. "Some hope of her ever comin' here."

"Shush!" the greybeard warned. "The judge'll hear ya." He winked at Pete. "He's out back having his siesta."

"So, he's the law round here?"

"Yep, and a purty good job he does, too."

"Yeah," the thin-faced man sniggered. "Remember when I shot that Chink? The judge reckon he couldn't find nuthin' in his law-book aginst shooting a Chinaman so he dismissed the charge. Me and him's been good friends ever since."

"You don't say?" Pete said, his voice no more than a harsh whisper, taking another swig of the bottle. "Sounds like a real impartial administrator."

"Sure is," the greybeard hooted. "Chuckawalla Slim here's his chief hangman and strongarm."

"You don't say?" Pete repeated, and poured the greybeard a glass of whiskey. "Judge, is he? Legally appointed by the state of Texas?"

"Hell no," the old guy protested. "He's only a justice of the peace. Got a few townspeople to elect him. At the point of a gun."

"Shuddup, you ole fool," Slim snarled. "He's got a law-book. He makes a good judge, don't he?"

Most of the men growled assent. "Remember that horse-thief?" one asked. "Judge Bean confiscated his horse, gear, guns and money and set him loose outside town under the threat of treading air if he returned. A wise decision. Man gets his hoss stole in this terrain means almost certain death. Gave that galoot a taste of his own medicine."

"Yeah" another put in. "They found his skeleton fifty miles out. Picked clean by the vultures. Sure saved us the cost of a burial."

"Sounds a real friendly town. Anybody got a set of cards?"

Slim's eyes gleamed at this, as they had done when he had seen the double eagle, worth twenty dollars, put down by the stranger. Eyes that had an unblinking obsidian greed. No wonder they called him Chuckawalla. He looked like a lizard. He nodded to two of the *hombres*, gave a thin-lipped smile. "What's it to be? Poker?"

"Suits me," Pete said, ambling over to a table with the men. He poured them all a shot from the bottle. "Deal me in, gentlemen."

★ ★ ★

Maybe he shouldn't have started on the hooch. He could feel it getting to him, his mind hot and spinning. Maybe

9

he should have kept his cool, ignored their blatant cheating, their threatening attitude, cut his losses, moved on out of Langtry. He didn't need any more trouble. He had had trouble enough. It swung up at him still —

the leaping flames, the screams, the shouts, the whinnying horses, the crashing timbers as his wife and his friend, her friend, her lover, were burned alive, the invaders howling their hate, too many for him, hauling him up to hang his neck from the entrance gateway of his Wild Rose ranch, the rawhide burning him, choking him until they had gone and his young son climbed up to cut him down. And staring aghast into the flames. His life, their life, gone. And in the morning burying the bloody charred bodies.[1]

Would the memory always swing up at him like a burning brand thrust into

[1]See Death at Sombrero Rock

his face, into his mind? Maybe it was this that made him feel mean? He had had enough of no-good men trying to skin him. From now on he would take it from no man, for death would be a spectre beside him. He did not need to. These three scumbags were trying every trick in the book to gull a man they obviously took for some wandering saddle-bum. He had already parted with thirty dollars he could ill afford. Maybe the whiskey had made him dozy, but it had slowly dawned on him that these three did not intend him to get out of there with his life, let alone his money. A cold shiver went through him as he looked around the gloomy saloon.

They had him set up. Who else was there waiting to gun him?

"Strikes me this is the crookedest game I ever stepped into," he whispered, in his hoarse tone, and a smile like the pained snarl of a mountain lion.

Cold lizard eyes across the table registered his own. Killer's eyes. A predator. A man who knew he was cock of this particular dungheap. Probably a pretty fast gun. Sure of himself. And with a winning hand, for he had two evil-looking *pistoleros*, one on either side, to back him. The lizard mouth opened into an insidious grin: "What you talking 'bout, man?"

"I'm talking about you, you greasy-haired stinking sonuvabitch. You're dealing off the bottom of the pack and these two dingoes are helping you do it."

Chuckawalla Slim slowly spread his hands and three aces on the deck and calmly pulled his grey frock-coat back to reveal the heavy Colt Lightning .45 self-cocker hanging down across the front of his lap. Shiftily, his eyes went from side to side to check his *compagneros*, and back to meet Pete's glowering coal-black ones. "You sure are a bad loser, stranger," he jeered.

The two *hombres* were scraping their chairs back, getting to their feet. The hand of the big one in the green check shirt was scrabbling to open his buttoned-over army holster. The one with the heavy mustache was pulling a sawn-off from his overcoat pocket.

"Yeah, and you're lousy cheats" — Pete raised his open hands to show he did not want trouble — "Jest gimme back what you took offen me and we'll call it quits. I'm ridin' outa here."

But Chuckawalla had pulled out his Colt and he *was* fast. The nine-inch barrel was grinding smoke and flame and spewing death. Pete ducked as a blunt-nosed bullet scorched his temple, the force or shock of it knocking him backwards, and just as well, for four companion slugs splintered the bar behind him.

The almost-empty whiskey bottle toppled from the table on top of him and Pete caught it with his right hand to send it spinning at Mustache. It caught his jaw and he stepped back blamming the sawn-off, riddling the ceiling.

Black gunsmoke[1] wreathed the already gloomy saloon. Pete took advantage of it to roll away across the floor, pulling his left-hand Smith and Wesson as he did so, coming up on the far side of Chuckawalla Slim, kneeling, arm outstretched and unwavering, pumping one, two, three, four bullets into him in half that number of seconds, sending him spinning to collapse against the wooden wall, his lizard eyes becoming opaque, his Lightning clattering from his numb fingers. Chuckawalla slowly slid down to the floor leaving smear-lines of blood on the wall above him.

Check Shirt had his revolver raised and was seeking him through the smoke. His slugs smashed glasses on the shelves. One bullet caught Lily

---

[1]There would have been a lot of black powder smoke at this time, a fact often overlooked by Hollywood directors. Smokeless cartridges, a French invention, did not appear until 1885.

Langtry in her belly. Pete swung his extended arms toward him, a double-hold to steady his aim — 'BOU-woum!' — the man was bowled back, a small red hole appearing in his forehead.

Sawn-off loosed his second barrel as Pete rolled for cover once more — 'BLAM'! — the scatter nearly parted his hair. The idiot had played his hand. Pete could have let him be, but he didn't want to. He felt meaner than a gut-shot grizzly. He despatched him from close range making a mess of his minimal brains. The fellow had put them to poor use for the final time.

"Anybody else want it?" Pete gritted out, but the onlookers were awed and silent, their ears ringing from the explosions. The cowboy pocketed the cash on the table. "All I wanted was a friendly game of cards. They didn't need to drink all my durn red-eye."

"Jeez!" Greybeard hooted. "Didja ever see shootin' like that? Ole Chuckawalla sure got his aces back in the hole. Four of them, straight into his heart."

"These men drew on me," Pete said, backing away, pulling his hat down tight, his right-hand revolver sweeping the watching circle, glancing around, ready to make a run for it, feeling behind him for the door.

Too late he saw the greybeard gawping over his shoulder. A heavy thud juddered the back of his skull, knocking him forward, his knees sagging, his mind exploding. He crumpled slowly over and looked up, momentarily aware of a big, bearded man stood over him, rifle butt poised, ready to buffalo him again, and he knew it was Judge Bean . . . before darkness closed over him.

2

BLACK PETE woke in a black hole. Pitch black. All he could make out was rounded stone walls, and a sandy bottom he was laying on. He reached up to feel a throbbing lump at the back of his head. It was matted and sticky: blood. And there was blood trickling from the bullet graze on his temple. He groaned, not only with pain, but dismay. What a durn fool way to go! The only good thing was that he had sent his money from selling the herd and horses, from what he had made as a lawman, the reward on the Doolin brothers, several thousand dollars, by banker's draft to Kansas to the boy's aunt. They wouldn't be able to rob him of that before they . . .

A wooden lid was suddenly scraped back to reveal a circular section of starry sky against which several heads were silhouetted. "Toss him in," a voice grated. And a young man was hurled, kicking and scrabbling, down on top of him. By the gleam of light Pete saw that his visitor was dressed as a nondescript cowpoke, before their hole was sealed by the board and, by the sound of it, a great boulder rolled on top of it.

"Howdy," Pete croaked, striking a match and lighting the stub of a cheroot he had found in his pocket. "What brings you here?"

"I guess I got a little drunk and took a poke at the jerge" — by the light of the match Pete saw the cowpoke give a goofy grin — "You must be the fella that done shot up the saloon."

"Yep. I guess I am."

"Them three needed killin'. But they gonna hang ya."

"Yep. I guess they are. What about you?"

"Hoots! I got a plan. I gonna fool thet ole Judge Bean. But you, they

18

gonna hang you. I heard 'em say so. So you better start sayin' your prayers, stranger, 'cause I don' reckon you'll make it past them pearly gates. You'll mo' like frizzle in hell."

"Yep. More'n likely. What's your plan?"

"You know thet actress, Lily Langtry? I'm gonna tell the judge I met her in Chicago, that I'm a friend of her'n, and maybe I can persuade her to come and visit this lil ole town."

"Yeah, well, you work on your plan. Me, I'm gonna say my prayers and try and get some shut-eye. OK?"

With that, Pete rolled over and growled, "And mind where you're steppin' next time they throw you in here."

★ ★ ★

It must have been midday when they came for them. The sun was high and blazing hot. They didn't have the decency to give them a cup of

19

coffee or even a mug of water before they tied their wrists tight behind them with rawhide and marched them along to the Lily Langtry saloon. Judge Bean, in a giant sombrero, sat in state on a beer barrel on his shaded veranda. Half a dozen men lined up on horseback on either side of the saloon front. They were, Pete presumed, the jury.

"Put Matthews up first," the judge ordered, scratching at his big pale belly through his open shirt. "Drunk and disorderly, abusive language, and assault on my person. Very serious charges. What have you got to say for yourself, Matthews?"

The cowpoke, aware that Bean might very well confiscate his horse in lieu of fine, began to snivel and snuffle, saying he just didn't know what came over him, he wasn't used to whiskey. The judge looked unimpressed. He took up a straw-bound gallon jug of rum and took a long swig over his shoulder. And had the jug passed to the jury.

"How about one for the prisoners?"

Pete asked, but they ignored him, although a few scraggy women and kids who had come to watch gave snorts of laughter.

"Order in court!" the judge shouted, banging his revolver as a gavel. But he had begun to cock an ear to the cowpoke's story, his pale-blue eyes getting a far-off misty look in them. "Is that so? Lily? You wouldn't be lyin'?"

"Swear it on my mother's grave, judge. That Lily Langtry's the most beautiful creature I ever set eyes on. The gentlest, the . . . I saw her at the Chicago music-hall. As pure as a dove, you can tell that — "

"Really?"

"She's jest a high-class hoo-er," Pete growled (for although he had nothing against Miss Langtry he was feeling real mean towards the judge). "It's a well-known fact she goes down on that idle bladder of English lard the Prince of Wales."

"What?" Judge Bean was so amazed

21

his voice came out more as a squeak than the intended roar. "What did you say?"

"You heerd. Nor's she so wonderful in the looks department. Someone told me she's got a squint and a wooden leg. Or is that Sarah Bernhardt? Both a couple of painted prostitutes. Not that they'd have anything to do with a rum-soaked stinkin' old twister like you."

"Wha-at?" Judge Bean squeaked, pulling out a filthy bandanna to wipe his brow, and beckoning desperately for the jug to be passed back his way.

"She ain' nothin' like that, Judge. I seen her."

"OK, Matthews. I want you to tell me everything she said to you. Everything about her. Put him in the back room, boys. Untie him. First I gotta deal with this . . . this scurrilous villain . . . this triple murderer who shot down poor Slim and his friends in cold blood. What do you say? Are you guilty?"

"Nope. You're the one who's guilty,

you drunken warthog. You set those boys up to rob me and shoot me down. No doubt you prey on all strangers who pass this way. I demand to be taken to Lawson for a fair trial. This phoney set-up . . . this ain't no court."

Judge Bean's face had become beetroot-coloured. He looked about ready to have apoplexy. He hammered his revolver on his table at the giggling gaggle of onlookers, waved his big battered law-book. "Silence! This court is officially recognized by the Texas Rangers. What I say is law. Understand?"

"Baloney!" Pete whispered, and spat into the sand. If they were going to hang him anyway, he might as tell them what he thought. "The Rangers only tolerate you handing out so-called justice to line your own pockets because it saves them coming all this way to pick up a few no-good rustlers. I should know. Hell, I've been a lawman."

"Lawman?" Judge Bean looked perplexed. This tall lean stranger with the hard black eyes and hoarse voice had got him rattled. "What kinda lawman?"

"Marshal of Abilene and of Dodge. Judge Parker — a real judge, not a phoney one — up at Fort Smith ain't gonna like this. You interferin' with me. So happens I'm on a mission for him."

It was a bluff, based on the truth. Black Pete had served as a US Deputy Marshal. He was counting on news of his killing cattleman Murchison not having filtered through to Langtry yet. The telegraph line and railroad had not yet reached this town.

Murchison was responsible for the murder of Pete's wife but a man couldn't expect to walk into the San Antonio Cattleman's Club and kill a Texas cattle baron and get away with it. Was Bean, he wondered, aware that there was a large price on his head? If he was he had no chance.

"Bring out the corpses," Bean shouted, as if in need of a diversion. And the

24

bloody bodies of Chuckawalla Slim and his sidekicks were dragged out. "How much cash has Slim on him?"

"Let's see, about ninety dollars," one of the men said. "Whewee! He don't half whiff! And look at this! He's got a lil derringer in his boot."

"Right! I fine that corpse ninety dollars for carryin' a concealed weapon and stinkin' up the place. Put it in my till and get him outa here."

"This is ridiculous. This ain't no court. I'm warning you, Bean — "

"Did you put them bullets in that corpse?"

"I've told you. In self-defence."

"That's true. They drew their guns on him," the old whitebeard suddenly blurted out. "He's innocent, judge."

"Throw that idiot outa my court," Judge Bean roared, hammering on his table. "What do the jury say?"

The men mounted on their cowponies shrugged and one by one gave the thumbs down sign.

"You heard that old man, Bean.

You better untie me. Washington ain't going to look kindly on this."

"Black Pete, or whatever your damned name is, I sentence you to be hanged by the neck until you're dead for the murder of Chuckawalla Slim and his two *amigos*, whose monickers escape me. How much has the prisoner on him?"

"Thirty dollars and a watch."

"I also fine you thirty dollars, a watch, and confiscation of your horse and guns for insulting and lying about a lady. Go get his hoss, boys. We'll let him go in style."

When the saddled-up grey was brought from the livery, Pete was hoisted up onto her and the judge intoned, "And may the Lord have mercy on your soul, young man. Take him to the hanging-tree, boys."

The filly had been taught to stand silent at the sight of a rattlesnake, to cut a ferocious longhorn out of a herd, to numerous words of command. "Hee-yaaagh!" Black Pete screamed, which was his command for trouble, for the filly to rear and spin and kick and buck. And he was free, the people around him scattered into the dust. He kicked the filly with his spurs to send her galloping away out of town as he hung low over her neck, his wrists tied behind him, as lead whistled past his ears.

"Go there, gal!" he shouted as she surged forward, her mane flying in his face.

3

THE young filly was breathing hard, wild-eyed, white spittle clinging to the sweat streaming from her sides as Black Pete urged her on with a jab of his spurs and a whack across her haunches from a quirt hanging from his wrist. The horse was all but done for. He did not normally punish her (and, in fact, had filed down the vicious rowels of his Mexican spurs out of respect for her) but it was the only way if they were to survive. For a day and a night he had been pushing her at a fast pace across waterless desert, ninety merciless miles of scrub and sand. It was the only way to get through the *Journada del Muerto*, the Journey of Death, by going at a non-stop determined lope (and hope not to come face to face with any Apaches en route). The Murchison boys had put a thousand-dollar price on his head, and the Rangers, or bounty-hunters, would be on his trail. This was the only way to shake off pursuit. Few men were willing to attempt this journey. At high noon the previous day he had given the horse the last of the water in his canteen, letting her nuzzle it from his palm as they rested for a brief respite in the shade of a rock. They had ridden on and on through the night and now it was almost dawn. No, she didn't look good. She was blowing and unsteady on her feet. He winced as he put her to the whip. It was the only way.

She had certainly saved his neck at Langtry. One hanging in a man's life was enough. She had kicked out and pulled away from their captors, and as she charged out he had managed to pick up the reins with his teeth and keep her on course for many miles. The men of Langtry had made a half-hearted effort to get a posse up and follow him, but they didn't have a lot of enthusiasm for the chase. And who could blame them in that hundred degree heat. Pete had cut his ropes free on a sharp rock and shown them his dust. That robbing bastard had got Pete's weaponry, the superb revolvers, and the latest modern Winchester, that year's model, a .73, had taken his knife and his cash, but had let a thousand-dollar reward slip through his fingers.

He had been tempted to turn south-west and head up into the great wilderness of the Chisos, stronghold of Mescalero Apaches and haunt of eagles, lions and rustlers, but he had no wish to hide out there for the rest of his life. So, he had gone north-west into New Mexico, taking this terrible short cut. He regarded the horse anxiously. He had no wish to lose her. He had spent three years gentling her. He had intended her to be his son's mount, but she had outgrown him. She was no ordinary mustang. He had brought her in from the wild, but she had the Roman nose of a Spanish thoroughbred, and the delicacy and grace and colouring of an Arab. One of her ancestors must have been owned by some proud conquistador, or maybe even ridden by a Moor. She was fast and agile. She did not have the staying power of Nimrod, his black stallion, who had been shot from under him in Indian Territory two months before he returned home. But the filly was too fast for that posse. By the time he had reached the frontier between Texas and New Mexico the chicken-hearted creeps had already turned back. The problem was he was out there in the wilderness without any weapons. If he didn't meet any lawmen, killers, Comancheros or prowling Mescalero, he had nothing to contend with lesser hazards.

These were by no means minimal. If a man lay down on his bed-roll in this desert country he was likely to encounter anything from eight-inch blue and orange centipedes with toxic mandibles, kissing bugs which could cause nerve damage, to black widow spiders that had the ability to give a man lethal muscle cramps. The main danger, though, came from rattlers, with their heat sensing mechanisms. Not so much to him, he could fend them off with a forked stick. But to his horse. And without a horse in that country a man was as good as dead. That was why they always strung up horse-thieves.

Nonetheless, Pete had been running wild since the age of seven, being brought up by farming folk in the woods of East Texas, and in the nineteen years since then he had learned the tricks of survival. At the age of fifteen he had gone off with the Texas Volunteers to fight for the Confederacy in the big conflagration and had learned more about killing than any boy ought to know. By the end of the war he had looked on the bodies of dead men laying by the side of the trail with as little compunction as for the hogs that fed on their bodies.

As he rode through the night it all came back to him, the ruination of the South, the collapse of an ordered way of life, the harsh taxes imposed by the Northerners on all who had supported the rebellion, and along with that the famine, the floods, the plagues of locusts, the long fierce droughts, the fires, the epizootic disease among horses, the Texas longhorn fever, scurvy, consumption and cholera all adding their toll to the pestilence of war. He had worked and fought to raise a herd on his land and for a few years it seemed they had won through. He had led a cattle drive to Dodge only to see the depression that recently swept the whole country, the failure of the banks, wipe him out. He had stayed on as a deputy marshal to raise more money, but in the year that he was away his wife, Louisa, had taken his friend as her lover. He did not know which was the biggest shock, discovering that, or hours later when the Stranglers attacked and she burned. It was the ruination of him, that was for sure, of all that he had lived and worked for. Sometimes it seemed he had been riding and fighting all his life, and for what? He hadn't even a dollar in his pocket. He would have to start all over again. But how could he, when he was a hunted outlaw?

The sun was glimmering over the edge of the waterless plain and through the morning heat mist he could see the blue outlines of a range of hills getting near. They had made it! He patted the filly's neck and slowed his pace. "We're there, gal," he muttered — he had never got round to giving her a name. "We're going to take it easier from here on."

And, indeed, they did. It was good to reach the fast-flowing Rio Grande and a region of rich grama grass up to the horse's belly. Pete let the horse have her fill, for, unlike most men who regarded a mustang as little more than a brute tool, over the years he had developed a great sympathy with the animal. One night he put in at a ramshackle farmhouse, half dug-out and half sod-built, a cow grazing on its roof. The staring-eyed Scotsman shared a flea-infested bed with his wife, two daughters and three snot-nosed boys. Also, no doubt, with any wandering scorpions, snakes, or skunks. A surly, catatonic mob, but they shared their water and supper with Pete as was the custom of the West.

"What would be the reason you are not carrying any weapons?" the Scot asked suspiciously eyeing Pete's empty holsters.

"Got dry-gulched by a couple of roughnecks way back," Pete drawled, as he chewed on stewed goat. "Managed to fight 'em off, but had to leave my guns behind."

"Hrmph!" the Scotsman snorted. He had taken an interest in Pete's saddle, with its silver horn, which he had taken from a Comanchero down in Mexico. "I'll trade you a rifle and a Colt revolver for yon saddle. And a box of bullets to go with them. If you're crossing the Animas range you may well be needing them. It's infested with smugglers and outlaws."

Reluctantly, Pete agreed. The Colt revolver he received was an ancient model, its walnut butt half eaten away by termites. And the rifle was a seven-shot Spencer, veteran of the Civil War, and probably the Mexican war before that. He was glad of the weapons, though. As he oiled them, loaded them, tried their feel, for the first time since quitting Texas he felt safe. Well, as safe as a man could be among the killers who roamed this land. The Rangers had a reputation of always getting their man. They might be unwilling to follow him across the state line, and through the Journada del Muerto. You never knew with those old boys though. Some of them just hung doggedly on and on . . .

Pete declined the Scotsman's offer to join them in their bed, preferring the company of rats in the barn. In the morning he wished them well and set off riding bareback, his bed-roll tied across his shoulders along with a small sack of flour and beans the Sotsman had given him. But with a revolver on his hip, and the rifle balanced across the filly's neck, and with a good rest and food inside him, he felt more ready to take on the world.

No, he was not so much worried about the possibilities of meeting lawmen. Or even Indians. The Mescaleros had been subjugated by Colonel Carson's fire and were on a reservation further north. Now and again a few of the young Messys took a notion to go on the warpath but he reckoned he could handle them. Over in the adjacent territory of Arizona, where he was headed, the Army were chasing Geronimo and his Chiracahuas, but that was mostly in the mountains further south. They were not the main danger. That came from his own kind. There were some mighty odd folk heading west these days, more since the big war than at any time before. Former slaves coming west or deserting from the all-black Army regiments. Sodbusters claiming their 160 free acres, trying to plough a living from the hostile land. Nesters creeping in, rustling stock, in constant conflict with the big cattlemen. Wild footloose youngsters from the east who rode the rails of the puffing billies that now crossed the continent. Fugitives from justice, former guerillas, the driftwood of the territories, who joined forces with outlaws and smugglers in killing and looting all who crossed their paths. It was a highly explosive mix of national and racial tensions, fuelled by whiskey and the cheaply available six-gun. No wonder the Navajos hid themselves away in their pueblos high in the mountains!

Such thoughts kept Pete constantly on the *qui vive* as he made his way through the Animas valley in this remote south-west corner of New Mexico and took the Skelton Canyon route, winding through the rough red cliff gorges of the Peloncillo Mountains. But he saw little signs of humans, only their remains, or those of animals, the scattering of wind-bleached bones.

He had heard that silver had been found along the Rio Diablo and he had a vague notion of maybe reviving his fortunes. At twenty-six, he was getting weary of forever wandering. He had a hankering to settle down and start another little spread of his own. To forget what had happened and make something of his life. He would kill if he had to, but he had no wish to be a killer by profession.

Surely he could change his name and disappear into this vast half-explored territory. When he found somewhere safe he would send for the boy. He would do it for Louisa.

Black Pete crossed the hostile ranges without misfortune. The filly was back in full fettle, wild and fiery. Her spirit had never been viciously broken. One morning he rode out of one of the red cliff gorges and the grey's ears pricked up as she heard the gentle lowing of cattle, a sound she was familiar with for she had been trained as a cut-horse. Pete had only to say 'Geddit' and she would bound forward to cut some maverick out of the herd.

Pete slipped down from her bare back and knelt behind some rocks to take a look-see. A milling bunch of about a hundred longhorns was being coaxed along by four riders, Mexicans by the *vaquero* costume, the long ponchos and wide sombreros. They were herding the beasts towards a narrow but fast-flowing river that wound through the valley. It was a pleasant sight, the prancing horses and sharp cries of the men, the tossing horns of the trotting beasts, set against a background of countryside that was a melange of blues, pinks and yellows beneath a peaceful cloudless sky.

This must be the valley of the Rio Diablo. He guessed the silver-workings that had sprouted up under the glorified name of Diablo City were further upstream. This appeared to be an all-Mexican outfit, probably an ancient hacienda that had been there from before the US-Mexican war thirty years before.

He guessed there was no reason why they shouldn't let him pass through their land and he was about to jump on the grey's back and hail them when the sound of a rifle shot barrelled along the valley and he saw one of the *vaqueros* pitch from the saddle.

At the same time there was a yip-yipping and hallooing as a gang of more than a dozen men came charging down from the nearby hills, some with carbines at their shoulders, others loosing off six-guns. They were obviously intent on taking over the herd, which, alarmed, had set off at a lumbering run alongside the river, soon to become a dangerous stampede of horn and hide unless they were turned.

Another Mexican's head jerked back, his arms flailing wide as a bullet hit him in the chest, knocking him into a backward somersault. The other two drovers leapt from their mustangs and took cover among the rocks. They wouldn't have much chance of holding out there against such a gang of men. The herd was surely lost.

True to his Texan instincts Pete raised the Spencer rifle to balance on a rock and squinted along the sights. He jerked the lever and fed a .52 calibre bullet from the tubular magazine into the breech. He took aim on one of the leading riders. His finger began to squeeze the trigger. He hesitated.

"This ain't none of my business," he muttered. "How do I know them greasers ain't the rustlers? Aw, hell . . . " An instinct bred over years told him otherwise.

His first bullet took off the leading rider's hat. The Spencer, made in Boston in 1860, was firing a trifle high. But it made the rider duck down with alarm, looking around as he heard the explosion cracking off the hillside. The man swerved his horse, giving one of the *vaqueros* a chance to bring him crashing down.

"Shee-it!" Pete growled. "Why do I allus have to git involved?" But it was too late now. In for a cent, in for a dollar's worth. He pulled back the firing hammer with his thumb, ejected the empty case, inserted another heavy slug, and this time aimed low at the buckle of a man's belt. Split seconds later the slug ploughed through the man's throat and he was catapulted to the ground.

From his position on the cliffside, sheltered by the rocks, Pete was perfectly placed for sniper fire. Several of the men galloped their horses towards him to investigate, and three of them were sent flying to perdition by a rapid fire of .52 lead.

The others quickly dismounted and took cover. They kept their heads down as Pete's bullets chiselled the rocks. One of them foolishly exposed himself and Pete's lead took off the top of his head. A mess of blood and brains splashed over his companions.

Pete laid aside the empty seven-shot

Spencer and pulled the old Colt from his belt, hoping the relic wouldn't burst its seams and backfire on him. He'd known men lose a hand with such things. Anyhow, at a range of 150 yards it wasn't much use. He blammed away at the men on horseback who were harassing the two *vaqueros* just to let them know he was still there. He thrust the empty Colt back in his belt.

He had six slugs left in his mackinaw pocket to fit the Spencer. He reloaded, wriggled to another position in the sagebrush, aimed carefully, and with four shots took two men out of the saddle. That was seven of them he had accounted for.

There was a lull in the action. The men had begun to realize they were dealing with a marksman and one in a pretty unassailable position. It might take all morning to dislodge him.

What now? Pete had two cards left to play. He could spare one shot, maybe panic them while he had the advantage. The last bullet he would save for a final suicidal stand against them. The shot winged the arm of one of the riders. He was a burly, bearded man dressed in a flapping dust-coat and battered hat, who cried out with pain, clutched at the ruddy stain and called the men off.

Five men below Pete scrambled onto their horses as if the devil was after them and, cursing and flailing, set off at a gallop back the way they had come.

"Phewee!" Pete whistled with relief. "Durn fools. I only got one slug left. They coulda had me. Still, how were they to know?"

He picked up the rifle and waved it at the two *vaqueros* as they came out of the brush. "Not a bad ole shootin'-piece, this Spencer."

He jumped back onto the filly's bare back and, guiding her with the rope hackamore, for the Scotsman had taken his silver-embroidered bridle as well, he weaved his way down the cliff slope, letting the filly more or less find her own safest route. The two Mexicans on horseback came to meet him.

"You the lawful owners of them cows?" he asked, in the belligerent way that reflected his days as a lawman.

"*Si, señor,*" one of the Mexicans said. "Our *patron*, don Miguel del Rioja, will be proud to reward you for saving a valuable herd, not to say our lives."

"Too bad about your two *compagneros*," Pete said. "Where did those skunks come from?"

"Diablo City, *señor*. Many bad people live there now. We have much trouble."

"Pete is the handle. Less of the *señor*. Maybe I'd better help you two catch up with that herd or it won't be so valuable at all. Come on, geddit, hoss. *Vamos!*"

And he led them galloping off after the departed steers.

4

THE Rioja abode was more a fortified farmhouse with adjacent outbuildings of blacksmith's shop, wagon-maker's, bakehouse, dairy, stables, kitchens and bunkhouse built of thick flat-roofed adobe and rock, weathered by time, its corrals surrounded by high and ancient walls which glowed pink in the setting sun as Black Pete and the two *vaqueros* herded the longhorns in. A look-out clanged a bell and opened sturdy oaken gates to admit them.

"Looks like this place could withstand a siege," Pete muttered.

"It bin here more than hundred years," grinned one of the *vaqueros*. "Apaches, Confederates, Union troops don't dislodge us. But those rustlers, they another thing."

A stocky elderly man, with a shock

of white hair and a haughty jut to his aristocratic nose, dressed in *vaquero*'s worn leathers, ran from the house. "What's happened?" he asked.

"They got Joaquin and Tomás, *señor*. They came pouring down upon us, thirteen of them," the cheery *vaquero* replied, in Spanish.

"Who's this?" The old man eyed Black Pete. "A prisoner?"

"No, the *gringo* appeared from nowhere like our guardian angel. He killed seven of them, saved the herd."

"It might be worth sending a couple of men out to pick up the guns and ammunition of the dead. I'm right out of lead and all I got is this useless old antique" — Pete spoke in fluent Spanish, too, sliding down, extending a gloved hand. "Guess you must be *Señor* del Rioja."

The *haciendado* grasped his hand with both of his own and gave a strong grip. "*Señor*, I give you my thanks. Not only for saving my herd but for saving these men's lives."

48

"Jest happened to be passing by," Pete whispered. "Least I could do."

"And the least I can do is offer you the hospitality of my ranch," Rioja said, extending his arm towards his open doorway. He issued orders on the lines Pete had suggested, and for his grey to be cared for, and led him indoors.

They entered a flagged living area, it's three-foot thick walls keeping it cool in summer and warm in winter, where there were colourful Navajo carpets, a huge red stone fireplace, rifles stacked against the walls, a long banqueting table of polished oak, and great comfortable chairs cleverly devised of long-horns, leather and wood. Rioja pulled the corn-cob stopper on a flagon of *mescal* homebrew, and poured them a glass each. He raised his: "Once again, *gracias, señor*."

"The name's Pete."

"Where you headed, Pete?" Rioja slapped his arm and indicated a chair. "Looks like you have come far."

Pete brushed some of the red dust from his mackinaw, cast his hat aside, and pursed his lips as he tested the fiery liquor. "Yeah, a fair piece. Headin' for Diablo City."

"Ach! That place! A hang-out of thieves. We had a good life here before they found silver. For generations my family has ranched this land. I'm at my wits' end what to do. They are trying to drive us off. That's two more of my men murdered. Good *vaqueros* are hard to come by."

"Surely you know who they are? Can't the law help you?"

"Ha! Yes, I know who they are. Their leader is the law, or purports to be. A young killer we call *El Cuchillo*."

"The Knife?"

"Yes, an expert with knife, whip and gun. He has proclaimed himself sheriff of Diablo City. Nobody is inclined to argue with him."

"Not another one? I got dry-gulched by a buzzard like that back in Langtry. Seems like any son-of-a-gun who feels

50

so inclined is setting hisself up as the law."

"I don't think this one has the brains to be the boss of the outfit. He is — how you say — just a hoodlum. Somebody else is behind this campaign to ruin me, to kill us all."

Pete tipped back the *mescal*, stretched out his long legs and they both, in silence, pondered the injustices of life. "Can't the Army help out?"

"The nearest post is Fort Apache and they are too busy fighting the Chiracahuas to worry about me. We have to fight our own battles in this wild country, but" — he poured another glass — "forgive me, you must be starving."

He strode out to a kitchen area and spoke to a heavily-built Opata squaw, who appeared in the doorway. She was in long, rough, white woman's dress, topped by a pinafore, her dark hair pinned in bangs. Heavy silver ear-rings had stretched the lobes of her ears like plasticine. "One hour," she said, raising a finger.

Rioja returned with a bottle of rough red wine. "Maybe this is more to your taste. The Indians know how to cook venison. She will roast it slowly over the embers. I cannot hurry her."

"It will taste better for the waiting," Pete replied, trying to speak in the old-fashioned chivalrous manner of his host. The wine was old and good, of a rich ruby hue. He smacked his lips. "A good vintage, *señor*."

"One moment," Rioja said, going into an alcove that appeared to be his study.

He returned with a case which he opened to reveal a pair of Colt Frontiers lying in a velvet lining, with a spare cylinder, lubricant flask, and tools. The walnut grips were inlaid with silver replicas of eagles, their wings outstretched, instead of the customary colt rampant.

"For you. No, I insist. They are this year's model. I had them made by special order from Frankford arsenal. You see, they are centre-fire not rim-fire. A big improvement. Two hundred copper cartridges to go with them."

Pete gave a whistle through his teeth with awe as he handled one of them. "Serial number one," he said. "The very first." He put it back. "No, I cain't accept this."

"I want you to" — Rioja's dark face appeared to pale as he pressed the guns back to him. "They were for my son, Raoul. El Cuchillo killed him. He went into Diablo City against my wishes. He was hot-headed. He wanted to call this El Cuchillo to account. They shot him in the back."

The *haciendado* swallowed and looked quickly away, blinking away the tears that had started to his eyes. "Forgive an old man," he said.

"Waal," Pete drawled, a mite embarrassed, for he did not want to be beholden. He didn't want to get involved in another war. He wanted to get on his horse and get out of there.

He didn't want this Mexican thinking he could adopt him as his proxy son. Or even his hired gun. He would finish the bottle, have a meal, and go. "They're mighty fine. *Muchas gracias.*"

He picked out a leaflet from the box and chuckled. "Hey, listen to this. 'Treat these weapons well and they will treat your enemies badly. You have six friends in each of them.' Ole Sam was some salesman."

"Sam? Who is Sam." A girl's voice startled Pete, who looked up at a slim apparition, raven-haired and dressed in riding outfit. "I hear there has been trouble."

"Yes, and there would have been more if this gentleman had not happened along. Pete, this is my daughter, Juanita."

Pete stumbled to his feet, a revolver in his hand. "Ha!" he stuttered, tipping the barrel to his brow. "Howdy."

The girl's violet eyes met his, but she did not smile. "Is Pete going to work for us?"

"No, he is going to Diablo. Unless, that is," her father said, "he wishes to stay."

"Waal, mebbe . . . " Now that he had met her he wasn't so sure he was in such a hurry to mosey on. "Mebbe I could best help you people by offering my services to this El Cuchillo and find out jest what's goin' on."

5

THE off-key clarion call of a bugle horn blown by a man riding shotgun announced the arrival of the Butterfield Overland stage as the six-horse team came wheeling into Diablo City. The driver, his face and clothes wreathed with white dust, his old hat flattened back at the front, hauled back and dragged the horses to a halt outside the Silver Nugget saloon.

"Thar yar, gents," he hollered, jumping down. "Ah tol' ya we'd make it. All the way from Los An-ger-LEES. Yassuh! Ah tol' ya them Apach' wouldn' git ya. No need to go messin' ya pants. OK? Any folks for El Paso? Ah'm headin' out five pee emm with a fresh team. Sho, mistah, git ya tickets in the office, pronto."

Billy Joe climbed out of the stagecoach,

spun around dizzily, and immediately fell on his backside. Rough-looking men standing on the wooden sidewalk guffawed. Another tenderfoot had hit town. Billy Joe's curly-brimmed bowler tipped over his nose. He righted it, struggled to his feet, staggered as if inebriated, and brushed down his city suit. Ten days being tossed around like a pea in a bucket in that contraption had made his legs as rubbery as if he'd been on a long sea voyage.

He hurried to retrieve his carpet-bag, dentistry equipment and gas canisters from the baggage sack. "Please, gentlemen, be careful," he chided as the would-be prospectors dragged out their picks, granite buckets, ropes and winches. "This gas could explode."

He would certainly be glad to be rid of their odiferous company. Jammed in among their ripe burly bodies all those days as the stage swayed back and forth he might just as well have been travelling in a pen of grunting pigs. And their lurid language! It had made him go hot under his celluloid collar. Wouldn't he be glad to find a decent hotel, have a bath, and get into some clean sheets!

Diablo City had become, it seemed, the magnet for all the scum in Arizona Territory since Horace Higgins, a poverty-stricken nester, digging in his onion patch alongside the Rio Diablo, had found a silver nugget the size of his fist and had been foolish enough to announce it to the world. Some said the strike might rival that of their not-far-off neighbour, Tombstone, and from a population of thirty Diablo had proliferated overnight into a 'city' of some one thousand souls. If souls they had? Billy Joe was not sure about that as he despondently surveyed the scene.

The main drag was a maelstrom of churning wagons, recalcitrant mules hauling mining equipment, and scrubby unharnessed horses hitched to the rails. Hastily erected clapboard huts and half-built false-fronted stores leaned against each other, or tumbled up the mountainside. And there were crudely-painted signs for 'Dry Goods', 'Livery', 'Billiard Hall', 'Barber Shop', 'Nuggets Bought', or simply 'Nellie's'.

The Silver Nugget was the main saloon and cathouse, screams and shouts and the tinkle of a piano issuing from its half-open doors. Unkempt, bleary-eyed men staggered from the portals as if to testify to the strength of the liquor, or other sinful pursuits.

Billy Joe had been brought up in a fanatically Roman Catholic household, the fear of hell-fire, brimstone and eternal perdition drummed into him from an early age by his well-to-do parents. They lived in a mansion on San Francisco's Nob Hill, and if anything his mama had been over-protective, insisting until he was the age of six, upon dressing him in skirts and pantalets, and curling his long brown hair into ringlets. Under her poetry-quoting patronage he had become a somewhat sensitive boy.

His father on the other hand was a

remote martinet, fiercely disapproving of his son as a 'milksop'. He had made his money in the California gold-rush of '49. When Billy Joe reached the age of sixteen his father had insisted he should be thrown out into the world to earn his own living, become a self-made man like he had been. He had relented enough to pay for a month's course in dentistry, as his wife wanted her son not to have to soil his hands but to become a professional man. Mama had shed profuse tears when her husband had shown them the headline in *The Chronicle* about the bonanza silver-strike on the borders of Arizona and New Mexico Territory. Instead of urging Billy Joe to 'go West, young man', he had suggested south-east was the direction their son should take if he wished to prove himself. He had bought him a berth on a schooner going along the rocky coastline to Los Angeles, and provided enough for a ticket on the stage to Diablo City. Mama had chipped in a little more.

Diablo City had one advantage over more established mining-towns. Any penniless hopeful could arrive, stake out a claim and start digging into the rock. Most of them tried to get as near to Henry Higgins' patch as they possibly could, but the more intrepid headed out into the hills.

Others, however, preferred to prey on the hard workers, jumping their claims if they showed any promise of riches, mugging men down alleys, or shooting men in the back out at their mines and stealing what silver they had found. Some held up the stage, occasionally, and robbed the prospective prospectors before they had even reached town. The city was 'wide open', as they say.

"Well, here I am," Billy Joe said. "The promised city." It looked more like a nest of disturbed ants, as the workers in their dusty denims and dungarees hurried back and forth to the ramshackle diggings that pocked the hills like cheeseholes, and the drones sat around in the bars, or on barrels on the sidewalks unconcerned. A pall of dust hung over the place, and there was a sweet, foetid odour, a mixture of horse-droppings, burning horn from the smithy, *frijoles* being fried, tarred rope, unwashed bodies and human excrement.

He fixed tight the stud in his by now soiled collar, adjusted his tie, picked up his equipment, and climbed up onto the rickety sidewalk, pushing through the jostling clamour of men as courteously as he might. He was terrible dry, so tentatively, he entered The Silver Nugget. He had never entered such an establishment before, nor, at his age, of sixteen, had liquor ever passed his lips. There was a motley collection of men, ragged miners, Mexicans in ponchos and baggy whites, hill-billies with long beards wagging, a couple of dudes in derbys and chequered suits, fat-gutted storekeepers, and an assortment of windblown Westerners, in bandannas, wide-brimmed hats and leathers, bandoliers of bullets around their waists, shooting-irons thrust into their belts. Most were playing or watching, with hypnotized dedication, games of monte or *chusas* at the tables, while others stood drinking at the long bar.

Billy Joe was a boy of medium build, a fleshy snub nose making him look younger than his years, his brown hair constantly falling over his brow in a fringe. He wiped it aside, and signalled to the barkeep and proprietor, a large, jolly-looking man with several chins, and long flaxen hair. A notice behind the bar stated his name as Fingal O'Rafferty.

"What's it to be?" the 'keep shouted, wiping his counter with a rag. He sported a celluloid collar and cuffs, bracelets around his shirt elbows, and a long apron. Above his aquiline nose his bright eyes watched the new arrival inquisitively.

"Have you a glass of soda-water?" Billy Joe asked politely.

Conversation in the bar stopped dead. They all turned to look at him. He felt like a choirboy who'd done something wrong in front of the altar. Something drastically wrong!

"What you think this is, a soda-parlour? You're in the wrong place, sonny. Unless you want a shot of whiskey in it?"

"Oh, no thank you," Billy Joe protested. "I'm a teetotaller. My family is strictly temperance."

"We shoot teetotallers in here," the 'keep roared.

Most of the men laughed, good-humouredly, and returned to their cards. But in the centre of the saloon a thin, weasel-faced youth leaned nonchalantly against the bar among a group of rough-looking men. He was dressed in a flat-brimmed black hat, a blue floral bandanna knotted at his throat, a white shirt beneath a shiny black leather waistcoat, and natty striped pants over his boots. In a holster on his hip was a big silver-embossed

Magnum .357, which carried the larger blunt-nosed bullets called manstoppers that could tear a man's or a beast's guts apart. He winked at his cronies, pushed himself off the bar with his elbows, and sauntered over to Billy Joe. "Hi," he said. "You new in town? What's all this clutter you got here?"

"This is my equipment. I've got a degree in dentistry. I'm going to open a surgery in this town."

"You are? You'll need a licence to operate, kid. That's five dollars you owe *me*. I'm the sheriff here."

"You are? Are you sure? You haven't got any badge," Billy Joe protested. "What proof have you of that — "

"Proof? Listen to the lil whipper-snapper. This is my proof" — he produced a vicious knife and touched the boy's throat lovingly. "So happens I was only recently elected. Haven't had time to run up a badge yet."

A giant of a man stepped over. His great pot-belly sagged over his gun-belt, and his half-shaven ugly features beneath his wide-brimmed sombrero cracked into a black-gapped grin. "Yeah, and I'm his deputy. We and the boys and a couple of these worthy citizens kinduv elected us, ourselves. Okay, half-pint? So, that's another five dollars you owe me."

"No, I'm not paying you," Billy Joe said, trying to press him away because the scent of whiskey and sweat was overpowering. "I'll pay the sheriff. Where's your office? I'd like a proper licence written out, and signed."

"Office? Listen to the lil sucker," the youth cried. "This is my office. So cough up your five dollars now."

"There's no need to be rude," Billy Joe said, but pulled out a roll of greenbacks and fumbled for a five. He had decided it might be best to cough up. He passed one to the youth with the long crooked nose and close-together eyes. He felt like a rabbit beneath the gaze of a stoat which was about to pounce.

"Give him a mescal," the youth said,

stuffing the note into his shirt pocket.

"Mescal? What's that? What's that worm in the bottle?"

"Sure, you have to be having that," O'Rafferty assured him as he poured a large glass. "It keeps it lively. Made from the cactus. Good for you."

Billy Joe was half-dead with thirst so he took a drink. Seconds later it was as if an explosion had rocked through his head and the room started to spin. But a pleasant warm sensation poured through him.

"Mmm! I like that. I'll have another."

"Drinks all round," the big-gutted man said, slapping him so hard on the back he choked on the drink. "It's the custom, you lil twerp."

Billy Joe parted with another five-dollar note and the men whooped to get their glasses filled. "Is he really the sheriff?" Billy Joe asked O'Rafferty in a lowered voice.

The fat saloon-keeper wiped a glass and muttered, "They call him El Cuchillo. His real name's Lucifer

Grattan, one of the greasiest little rats on the frontier. His sidekick's known as Big Jake. They think they run this town. You want to watch out for both of them."

"I'll remember," Billy Joe said, looking around at the crowded saloon. Among the men were sprawled several ladies in skimpy dresses and some of them were very odd-looking ladies indeed. One was so fat she seemed more like a collection of fleshy balloons. Double-barrelled Annie she was called, for reasons, to Billy Joe, quite obscure. One was skinny and old, darkly Hispanic, her eyes harsh as a raven's, outlined by thick kohl, a thin moustache above her cruel painted lips. A shrill giggle attracted his attention to another, a wiry negress in a tight silver dress cut low across her chocolate-coloured chest. She opened her mouth in a wide grin of brilliant white teeth and flashed her velvety brown eyes at him.

"How would ye be likin' my girls?" the Irishman said. "I brought dem all wid me when I was run out of New Orleans. Ach, I was glad to be seein' the back of that place, the fogs, the bells, the black people, the ghosts, folk dropping like flies from the yellow fever, the cannons booming, the transportations of the sick to the islands. If you can dodge a few stray bullets this is certainly a much healthier place."

"Yes, I do believe the air is very clear," Billy Joe agreed. "A lot of consumptives come west."

"Would ye be knowin' somet'in'? The proportion of males to females is ten to one in this desolate territory. An available female, young and pretty, is as hard to find here as a goblin in a bottle. So how about trying one of my gals?"

"Goodness no. That goes against my religion. I would have to be married. Or at least engaged."

"Really?" Fingal said, and muttered to one side, "We've got a queer one here."

69

Billy Joe was alarmingly aware that the negress had sidled up close, and was wriggling her buttocks into him, her long fingers feeling at his thigh. "Hey, excuse me, miss. Don't do that. Yes, you know *what*. I don't like it."

"Who me?" The negress spun around, fanning her splayed hand at her chest: "Why, ah do declare, lawdy me, where oh where do you get such strange ideas from, white boy?"

"*You* know. I'm not like that. So go away, please."

The black girl screamed with laughter. "Sugah! Yo' sayin' ah touch yo'? Ah don' see how ah' could help myself. Ooh, yo' so masculine. One of the butchest handsomest hustlers ah ever done seen."

"I'm not a hustler. I'm a dentist" — the negress's fingers were fluttering everywhere, feeling in his back pocket, dipping inside his frock-coat. "Please desist."

His mind was spinning from the strange drink, and with embarrassment as the whole bar turned to join in the fun, the humiliation of a prim and prissy mama's boy. As Billy Joe grabbed to cover one pocket and to prevent the creature tickling him below his belt, her fingers emerged from another pocket with most of his dollar notes stuck to them.

"Ooh, lookee here. I like yo' pretty boy. Yo' come along upstairs. I'll make it worth yo' while."

"Cut it out, Esmeralda," Fingal snapped. "Leave him alone. Give him his money back."

"Why, Fingal, I nevuh done say a derogatory word." The negress tossed an ostrich feather shawl around her neck and stuffed the notes into her dress top. "The boy wants his cash he knows where to find it. Now own up, which one of you crazy numbahs touched his tha-aye?"

"You did. Just give me that back."

"Oh yeah, yo' a big heavy numbah. A macho man, huh? This town better look out. This boy's gonna tame us."

"He can tame me any day," one of the other 'girls' called out, and they were closing in around him, leering, laughing, the painted faces, such raddled harpies, reaching out hands to touch him, pull at his clothes, as if they would undress him there in that bar. He was pulling away, flustered, struggling to escape.

"Cut it out, you whores" — Lucifer Grattan had stepped in between them — "this boy's a friend of mine."

"Lawdy! I do declare" — Esmeralda fanned a hand at her chest — "a friend of your'n. We didn't know."

But they were backing off as El Cuchillo gripped Billy Joe's shoulder and pushed him back to the bar. "Don't take no notice of them weirdo harpies. Have another drink. I like you." Billy Joe blessed him for the rescue and accepted another *mescal* and soda-water. "I don't suppose you know where I could find a bed in this town?"

"A bed?" Fingal said. "You'd need

a pouch full of silver to find a free bed in Diablo City. Most people bring their own tent."

"Oh, gee. This never occurred to me."

"Is it a dentist you say you are? Well, I reckon you could make a good living in this town. You will be needing a surgery. It so happens I own a place across the way. A pawnshop below with living-space above. You could turn the living-quarters into your surgery.

"What about the pawnshop?"

"A terrible misfortune. Some brutes broke in and smashed the poor pawnbroker's head in the other night. Shouldn't you be doin' something about that, sheriff? Folks are really incensed at the things that are happening."

El Cuchillo shrugged. "We're looking for whoever did it."

"I'm sure you are. I tell you what, Billy Joe. You seem a sensible boy. You run the pawnshop for me in your spare time and you can have the rooms above for a pittance. Say ten dollars a week."

"Ten dollars! Isn't that rather a lot?"

"Take it or leave it."

Billy Joe thought of the last ten dollars he had in his hatband. "I . . . I'll think it over," he said.

"Don't take too long."

"What is that stuff you got there, doc?" Lucifer Grattan asked.

"It's gas. The latest discovery. Makes you oblivious to pain. I could extract your tooth and you wouldn't even know it."

"Oh yeah? Who are you kiddin'?"

"I assure you it's so. Allow me to demonstrate. Just take a seat in this chair."

Lucifer looked dubious, but drawled, "Okay." And sprawled in the chair, grinning crookedly at his men.

The *mescal* was weaving sneaky thoughts through Billy Joe's brain and making him brave. He bustled about arranging the cylinders, attracting

74

the attention of the card-players. This would be a good advertisement for his business, as well as a chance of getting a bit of his own back on Lucifer. He adjusted the mask on Lucifer's face, turned the taps on, and whispered, "Breathe deeply. Relax."

At that moment, however, a man with a blood-stained arm, his long dust-coat made even more ragged by a gunpowder burn mark, burst into the bar, followed by five dishevelled cowpokes.

"Rioja's mob. They kilt eight of the boys," he yelled at Lucifer. "It was slaughter. They had some marksman hid up on the cliff. We couldn't do a thing."

But his words were ignored, for the nitrous oxide had taken hold of Lucifer and he was in another world. His eyes closed, he was giggling uproariously.

"What's the matter with you?" the man in the dust-coat shouted. "I'm telling you, they've hired some kinda gun-slinger. What we gonna do?"

Lucifer just cackled fit to bust. And the card-players began tittering, too, as they watched, infected by his laughter.

"It's laughing-gas," Billy Joe explained, for he had given Lucifer a good whiff of it. "He can't hear you." He bent over the scrawny youth and opened his jaws, peering into his mouth. "Ah, yes. Now that's a nasty one. I think that ought to be out." He took a pair of pincers from his coat pocket, kneeled on Lucifer, got a firm grip, and, with some difficulty, yanked a back tooth out, brandishing the bloody rooted object for all to see. "Got it."

Oh heck, he thought. I got the wrong one. Perhaps it was time to make his own discreet withdrawal. "Gentlemen," he cried, gathering up his gear, "I'm not going to charge him for that demonstration. But if any of you are in trouble I'm at your service."

As Billy Joe stepped out of the Silver Nugget he could hear El Cuchillo still hooting with hysterics like a hyena, and the men roaring with laughter at him, pointing at the bulge pressing out his thin trousers. Nitrous oxide had that odd side-effect. "He's got a secret weapon," one of them shouted.

"I hope Lucifer doesn't mind being made fun of," Billy Joe murmured as he tumbled out onto the sidewalk, his legs giving way beneath him.

★ ★ ★

Billy Joe looked up into the stern regard of a minister of the cloth, the Reverend Ebediah Spank, in a dark suit and white dog-collar, a big leather-bound bible in his hands.

"How dare you, boy?" the minister was whinnying at him. "How dare you enter that house of shame at your tender age? Such filth, such corruption in our fair town."

"Once fair town," a young lady's voice put in, and Billy Joe saw a pair of dove-grey bootees, grey skirts, leading to a white-frilled blouse covering an immense bosom, a pretty heart-shaped

77

face, blonde hair and blue eyes. Her breasts trembled with indignation as she spoke. "How dare you pollute it, sir? Speak up when the minister addresses you."

"I didn't know," Billy Joe whimpered scrambling to his knees. "I didn't know they were like that in there."

"I do believe he's been drinking, reverend. There's a funny look in his eyes. Oh, dreadful boy, have you no regard for your soul?"

"Torments of eternal Hell await you, boy," the minister shouted, placing a hand on Billy Joe's head, holding him down. "They are all damned in there. Whores! Satanists!"

"I didn't know. I didn't do anything. I got out as soon as I could," Billy Joe said, struggling to get up.

"Repent, boy. Repent your foul sins, before it's too late. Come to the Lord."

"I tell you I haven't done anything to repent of. I've just got into town. I'm desperate to find an hotel room, but there seem to be none spare."

"We must save this boy," the young lady said. "He must come home with us, Mr Spank. I fear he will fall into sin if he is not found suitable lodgings. Poor boy, he looks so sweet, so innocent. I think I believe his protestations."

Billy Joe was picking up his luggage. "I assure you it's true," he said, staring into saucer eyes the colour of California forget-me-nots and his head beginning to spin even more. She is an angel, he thought. Sent to rescue me. "Praise be the Lord!" he cried.

"Allelieu-yah!" Spank joined him, loudly ranting on about how Diablo City would soon be struck by lightning bolts. "It has become the Sodom and Gomorrah of the plains," he screamed. "Come away, Miss Prissy, we must not linger here. Bring the young gentleman along."

79

6

"**Y**OU will have to come to service with us," the minister said as Prissy ladled out mutton stew into wooden bowls.

"Oh, I couldn't do that," Billy Joe protested. "I am a catholic."

"What?" The Reverend Spank jumped back from the table aghast, as if he could see horns sprouting from the boy's head. "An idolator? A worshiper of painted statues? A disciple of the holy Roman strumpet strutting in her richness and panoply?"

"Oh, it's the pageantry and incense and the golden robes that I love. And the Latin. It's so . . . so theatrical. You should see our church in San Francisco. Such a magnificent altar and real stained glass windows."

"Yes, theatrical. The gaudy images. The prostitution of good plain religion.

You might as well sit in a hothouse in a scarlet cloak drinking brandy."

Billy Joe smiled. "That's quite a good way of putting it, sir."

"Gentlemen," Miss Prissy put in. "The mutton's getting cold. I'm as shocked as you, reverend, that we have an idolater with us, a papist. But, I'm hungry."

"Shocked? I am more than shocked," the Rev Spank muttered, sitting down and preparing to say grace. Billy Joe closed his eyes and heard him intone, "Bless this food, oh Lord, and guide this poor young sinner away from gaudy Roman practices into the true belief. Oh Lord, I promise you he shall come into Your fold. He shall become a Presbyterian."

"But, I can't do that," Billy Joe said. "I've been confirmed. I've kissed the bishop's ring."

"Kissed his ring! And did you grovel on your knees before that scarlet-robed creature?"

"It's the way I've been brought up,"

Billy Joe said, tucking into the grub with haste, in case they decided to throw him out. "Mama and Pa are very strong Romans. Why, they would cut me off from my inheritance if I forsook the high religion."

"Your inheritance?" Miss Prissy enquired, her mouth full of mutton, her fleshy nose twitching, her blue eyes seeming to swivel like Catherine-wheels at the word. "Are your parents wealthy, Billy Joe?"

"Pa made a million out of his goldmine. I guess I will inherit something when I'm twenty-one. But Pa wants me to prove I can stand on my own two feet first."

"Really?" Prissy said. "Have some more mutton, Billy Joe. I'm so glad you decided to come to these parts. We have so few young men of breeding, of good family, of . . . of . . . "

"Money the word you're looking for, Miss Prissy?" the reverend asked.

Prissy fluttered her lashes, stroked her blonde plaits. "Well, it helps to be able to live a decent life. And one can do so much for the poor."

"Do I take it you teach school, Miss Prissy?" Billy Joe asked, enraptured by her blazing blue orbs.

"Yes, the poor children of these ignorant emigrants, so under-nourished in their bodies and minds."

Billy Joe spooned up his gravy and recalled noticing the white-painted church, with its bell-tower, and the schoolhouse adjoining the cottage. "Are you relatives, may I ask?"

"No, we share this house for convenience. Miss Prissy acts as my housekeeper. All quite above-board. Nothing salacious about it, you know."

Billy Joe saw a tinge of pink glow about Miss Prissy's eyes as she smiled at him, and he suddenly felt a booted foot gently rubbing against his own beneath the table. This is what they call 'playing footsie', he thought, and returned the pressure.

The Rev Spank was a man of about thirty-five years, with strong, straight features, a prow of a nose, a fine set of teeth, and a jutting chin. A full mane of chestnut hair increased his 'horseface' look, and his pale green eyes rolled with a dreamer's gleam. He and Miss Prissy were both sitting opposite the boy, staring at him. The nudging of the boot against his ankle was very curious. Wasn't it a large boot? Much larger than the little grey bootees Miss Prissy wore?

"How about some apple-pie?" Prissy asked, piling up the empty bowls and taking them to the sink.

Billy Joe went hot under the collar for, far from ceasing, the foot-rubbing became more activated. He had been playing 'footsie' for ten minutes with the Rev Spank! He whipped his boot away as if it had touched hot coals.

The Rev Spank seemed unperturbed, tucking into his dried apple-pie. Perhaps it was just a nervous foot-twitch he had? Billy Joe was so exhausted by the long journey, the peculiar effects of the mescal, and the large meal, he could hardly keep his eyes open. And he was much relieved when Prissy said she would show him to his bedroom.

"I am sure we are going to be true friends," she whispered, huskily, as she gave him his candle in its holder and brushed past him to go to her own room along the corridor.

Billy Joe undressed absent-mindedly, noting how comfortable the large double bed looked against the wall. He was standing naked sponging himself down from the bowl of water on the dressing-table when the Rev Spank slipped into the bedroom.

"My, what a sylph-like figure," he said. "A veritable Narcissus. If only I could be so slim."

Billy Joe snatched up his nightshirt and pulled it over his head. The reverend sat down, matter-of-fact like, took off his collar and began to unlace his boots.

"No need to be so coy, Billy Joe. We are both men, after all."

"What are you doing here?" Billy Joe stuttered.

"What do you mean?" the clergyman replied. "This is the only bed there is. We have to share."

"Oh?" Billy Joe didn't like the sound of it. But, perhaps, as the reverend put it, it was all above-board. He had heard that in poorer families sometimes as many as six men shared a bed. Only he couldn't help thinking he would have felt safer among six.

The reverend was humming a psalm, taking off his collar and shift to reveal a silken white skin which ceased at the red circle of his neck. He suddenly put a hand out to grip the boy's knee, nearly making him jump through the roof. "You and I have got to be friends, Billy Joe. You must write to your father and ask his generous support of a most worthy charity that I run. It is inter-denominational, so . . . "

The man's wheedling words became just a haze in the boy's mind. There was something about his pale eyes, his down-turned mouth up close to him that was repulsive to him. He

86

froze under his touch.

"Strange how chilly these desert nights get," the clergyman was saying as he began to pull off his pants. "We must cuddle up close for warmth."

"Not me. Oh, no!" Billy Joe jumped up and began to struggle into his suit over his nightshirt. "I'm sorry, I can't. I've got to go. I get claustrophobic sleeping with somebody else."

"What are you doing, boy? You can't go now. You'll wake Miss Prissy."

"Just watch me," Billy Joe said, as he went clanking out of the door and down the stairs with his gas canisters.

He groped his way through the darkness, letting himself out of the house via a window. He walked back down the dusty main drag. Oh dear, he thought, this trip west is rapidly becoming a nightmare. There were a few late revellers in the Silver Nugget so he went in there.

"Waal, I doo dee-clay-ah!" Esmeralda shrilled. "Look who's hay-ah! You wanna share my bed, white boy?"

"Been havin' trouble with the Rev?" Fingal asked. "We saw ye go off wid him. Dat devil dodger's for always rantin' and ravin' outside my saloon. I've had my suspicions of him. He protesteth too much."

"I wouldn't say anything against a man of the cloth. Perhaps I was mistaken. But I couldn't stay there any longer."

"You want to move into your surgery?"

"Please." Billy Joe felt inside his hatband and produced ten dollars. "I'll open shop tomorrow."

"C'mon. I like you, kid. I've got an old chaise-longue out back I've no use for. You can use it for your dentist's chair until you get established. I'll give you a hand to carry it across."

"Thank you. I like you, too, sir."

7

JUANITA DEL RIOJA looked out through the iron bars of her bedroom window into the yard and saw the stranger, the dark-haired *gringo*, washing at the tank, a round-walled pool of water fed by a natural spring. His broad back, tanned by the sun, was turned to her and as he bent over to dip his head every taut-honed muscle rippled and shone. Although he was tall and strong, his waist had the slenderness of youth. He was barefooted, in worn and faded Levi Strauss jeans tight against his strong horseman's buttocks. She heard him snort like a horse, waterdrops splashing in rainbow hues as he swung his glossy hair out of his eyes. Juanita stood and slowly caressed with her fingertips her pale naked breasts, kneading their uptilted nipples, her mouth going dry.

For the first time in her seventeen years she was, she realized, sexually aroused by a man. The Opata woman banging the gong for breakfast brought her to her senses. She buttoned her white cotton embroidered blouse to her throat as Pete, too, pulled on his faded blue cross-over canvas shirt and pressed tight its studs. He sat on the tank wall to pull on his boots and Juanita smiled as she tied back her hair with a purple scarf.

When they met at breakfast, however, she gave him only a brief and modest glance, while her father called out "Good-morning," and ushered him into a chair opposite her. The Opata woman served him an inch-thick burnt steak with two fried eggs on top. "Eat!" her father ordered. "A man needs a good breakfast."

The Texan grinned through his dark beard, in a wolfish way, and drawled, "I generally jest take cawfee." But he took up his knife and fork and got stuck in.

"Coffee, too," her father said, pouring

a thick black brew from the pot and pushing forward a jug of fresh cream.

"This is what a young friend of mine would call superdacious" — he was thinking of Molly who he had hunted through Indian Territory two months before — and Pete studied Juanita as he chewed. She was the complete opposite of the cocky little Moll, kinda cool and aloof.

Miguel del Rioja pushed his plate aside and sighed. "Two more men dead. I don't know how we're going to cope. We've got those hundred cows to brand. I was hoping to round up others on the northern range but with El Cuchillo's brigands on the prowl I hardly dare leave the house unguarded."

Black Pete had the uneasy feeling del Rioja was hoping he might offer his services but was too courteous to ask outright.

"Surely they couldn't breach these walls?" he asked.

"I have hardly enough men to guard

the gates. With ropes they could soon scale the walls. To tell you the truth, Pete, I am looking for a good man to escort Juanita back to Old Mexico. I will stay here, make a last stand. I am not leaving. I am prepared to die fighting for my land."

"I am not leaving either," Juanita said, and her violet eyes intensified in colour as she met theirs across the table. "You will not send me away."

She had the fiery hauteur of her Spanish *aristo* origins, and Pete smiled to see the steeliness in one so young. "Maybe things ain't as bad as they seem," he said. "Surely you can round up a few more *vaqueros*?"

"It would mean a long journey to Tucson," del Rioja said. "I cannot afford to be away. What would there be to return to? These men are ruthless. I fear they will burn us down."

"Not if I'm still breathin' they won't. I'll give you a hand with the branding this morning. Then I'll go take a look at these Diablo City boys."

"You don't have to," she said. "Father, you must not embroil this stranger. It is not his war."

"I know it ain't," Pete whispered, and his face tensed. "But I been burned off my own land by greed and thuggery, and I don't intend to stand by and see it happen to folks like you."

* * *

All through the long hot dusty morning he worked with the *hacienda*'s depleted staff lassoing, throwing, and branding the steers and calves. There were some wild bulls to chase and the girl, as she did what she could to help, marvelled at the natural agility of this *gringo*, he and his grey seeming to work as one, cornering and cutting out the beast they wanted. He was a natural cowboy as good as any *vaquero*. And that was a compliment indeed. Why, she wondered, had he become a wanderer? For one so young he rarely smiled, his face set as if he harboured some dark secret.

It was gone noon before the work was done. A pall of red dust hung over the corral, and a scent of burning hair and hide was in the air. Juanita was applying *tecole* to the earmark of a calf to prevent maggots festering when she looked round to see Pete kneeling on his haunches and high-heeled boots beside her, removing an iron from the fire. His coals of eyes met hers and seemed to clamp her soul. His thin lips twitched in a slight smile and he said, "Guess thet lil critter's the last one." He pressed the burning brand into the hide as Juanita held the calf down. "There ya." He pulled the rope free. "Go join your ma." And the calf did so, sprinting away, her tail held high, mooing plaintively.

Juanita walked beside him back to their horses. He was a head and shoulders taller, and his stride was long and kind of rolling but she felt good walking with him. And when they both swung onto their horses and wheeled away in unison, it was as if they had a natural harmony, jogging back to the ranch-house. Her father was out on the range and the Opata woman had taken a bucket of vittles over to the hands. Juanita rustled him up some milk and a sandwich, and she felt strangely weak, breathless, to be alone, in such close proximity to the man. She could sense him watching her as he leaned against the kitchen table. She wondered, if he caught hold of her as she brushed past him, whether she would be able to resist. But he did not. Just slowly ate the sandwich and watched her with those burning eyes.

"Time for me to mosey on," he said, in his husky way.

"Please," — she touched his arm, she could not help it — "take care. The people in that town. They would cut a man's throat for a dollar. They are filth. They live in squalor. They have no morals."

"I doubt if they'll bring a blush to

my maidenly cheek" — he smiled as he met her eyes and gripped her wrist, before removing her hand gently from his arm. "It wouldn't be no good, Juanita, if it's what you're thinking, between you and me. I'm wanted. For killing a man. Any day now I might have to move on."

"But men get killed all the time."

"Maybe. But this one was kinda special. A rich cattle baron. They ain't gonna be in a hurry to fergit."

The Spanish girl bit her full lower lip, and blinked tears from her eyes. She turned quickly away, her skirt rustling, and left the house.

Pete shrugged and shook his head, ruefully. "Jeez," he muttered. "Thet was hard to do. One more second of her looking at me like that and I'd have put my brand on that filly."

He was tightening the cinch on his horse when Juanita reappeared. She was carrying a fine Mexican saddle, its leather finely worked, and its horn of engraved silver.

"This was my brother's. I want you to have it."

"Not you, too? What is this? You don't have to."

"Take it. It is no good to us any more."

He resaddled the grey and swung aboard. "Hmm!" he grunted, settling himself. "Silver guns and a silver saddle. I feel like a true *caballero. Adios, muchacha.*" He grinned, doffed his gloved fingers at her, and with a flick of the reins went galloping away.

8

ON the plaza of Diablo City three Mexican *viciosos* were being forced at gunpoint to mount a makeshift gallows as Black Pete rode his grey into town. A big crowd had gathered to turn the event into a festive occasion: men were firing off guns, anvils were being clanged, firecrackers set off; street pedlars were selling barley sugar, fruit, *frijoles*, and icing-sugar skulls, like the Mexicans did on their Day of the Dead fiesta; an accordionist was playing a reel, some silver-prospectors were drunkenly dancing, swinging one another for lack of a girl, and a couple of cowpokes were whirling their horses in time to the music. It was not often there was a hanging in Diablo.

Generally all manner of crimes, shootings, stabbings, rustlings, stage hold-ups, the rolling of drunks down dark alleys, or even horse-thievery, went unpunished. But the citizenry had demanded that an example should be made. The town's pawnbroker had been murdered in a dastardly manner. And these three *renegados* had had the temerity to try to sell the articles stolen to frequenters of the saloons, to most of whom it belonged in the first place. The town chemist was swiftly elected a judge, and the three killers given a swift trial. That the chemist was a mild-mannered German who spoke little English hardly mattered. What was the point of interrogating the prisoners if their guilt was blatantly obvious? And if they didn't understand chemist's Latin that was their look-out. El Cuchillo, self-elected sheriff, had decided it might give him more credibility in the Territory if he were seen to be upholding the law. At that moment he was supervising the hanging and trying to make the criminals stand steady on a rickety plank platform. This was no easy matter for one of the villains was in a state of mortal funk, trembling so much he was 'rocking the boat', rolling his eyes upwards and begging for mercy.

"Hang onto him, Hank," Lucifer snarled. "I wanna get these noose knots placed right."

The other two *bandidos* were made of sterner stuff, leering and horribly cursing their audience as they stood there, their hands pinioned behind their backs. Old haybags in poke bonnets brandished their fists at them from the front row and were shrillest in their demand to El Cuchillo to 'make the bastards swing'.

"So, you see, dear boy, this is the way justice is operated out here," Fingal O'Rafferty told Billy Joe when he explained the foregoing facts after they had bumped into each other at the hanging. "Lucifer has persuaded the judge that it would be a wise course to swear in some more of his boys as deputies. We don't want the army, or US law enforcement agencies nosing into the town's affairs, do we? It is essential that the citizenry should be seen to have elected law enforcers of their own. That nobody actually voted for our Mister Cuchillo and his gang is neither here nor there."

Black Pete hitched his grey outside the saloon and overheard the fat saloon-keeper, in his pink-edged grey suit, succinctly explaining the proceedings to the gauche-looking youth who wore a city suit, with a bowler on the back of his head. He paused on the sidewalk beside them and watched a parson in dark cloth, his bible open, intoning verses to the condemned: " . . . for he cometh in with vanity and departeth in darkness and his name shall be covered with darkness."

Suddenly there was a drumroll and a deathly hush. Big Jake guffawed as he pulled the platform away and the three bandits twitched and jerked as they kicked air, their heads snapped sideways, their tongues lolling out, as they choked to death. Black Pete winced, his hand going instinctively to his own throat. The crowd gave a bloodlust roar of satisfaction and the hubbub recommenced. The three killers appeared oddly peaceful and pious as they were left to swing.

Pete cleared his throat, spat, gave a shudder, and pushed into the Silver Nugget, followed by O'Rafferty and the boy, and a surge of others of the onlookers.

Fingal noticed the tall, dark-bearded man in the hard-brimmed hat, and a brooding menace about him made him hurry to serve him. "What's it to be, mister? Did you enjoy the hanging?"

"To tell you the truth," Pete drawled, his voice still hoarse from his own, "I ain't overfond o' necktie-parties. No way. Make it whiskey and a beer."

"How about you, Billy Joe? We're partners now. The pawnbroker didn't leave no will. You're his nephew if anybody asks. So everything in the shop goes to us. The poor fellow's ill-fortune has done us a bit of good."

"But that's not true, I'm not."

"You are now. Drink up."

"No, I can't. Miss Prissy wouldn't like it."

"Miss Prissy isn't getting it. Come on, gargle a wee drop of whiskey. It's a holiday."

"Looks more like some damn pool of hell," Pete said as he eyed the painted 'prairie nymphs' giggling and screeching in their dresses in one corner. "What the devil are they?"

"They are our entertainers, sir," Fingal smiled. "Two dollars a session if you care to indulge."

"Yes, but what are they? You sure they're wimmin?"

"That's for us to know and you to discover. You might be pleasantly surprised."

"Shee-it!" Pete said, taking his whiskey to go sit in a corner. "Not tonight, Josephine."

103

"What's this about Miss Prissy?" Fingal asked.

"We're planning to be married."

"Married?" Fingal roared. "You mean that teacher, that fat girl with the simpering smile, she who thinks she knows better than anybody else? She who is holier than thou?"

"You are talking about my fiancée, Mister O'Rafferty. If you wish us to remain friends . . ."

"Oh, don't be silly. You're a mere boy. You can't be serious. Miss Prissy, eugh! She is so . . . so . . . bouncing, so horribly nice, so revoltingly cheerful, so off-puttingly good."

"She is a trifle on the large size, yes, I admit. But nice, cheerful, good, yes, she is. That's why I've fallen in love with her."

"Beware. Don't." Fingal pointed a finger at the boy. "Fall out of it as quickly as you can."

"She's already accepted me. Well, it was her idea. I wouldn't have dared ask. Apparently if it's a leap year that's all right. I've sent a letter on the stage asking Mama and Pa for their permission."

"What's this country comin' to?" Pete muttered, stretching out his long legs. "Used to be a place for *men*."

Scallywags and milk-sops, pick-purses and mughunters[1], thieves and city slickers of every denomination were flocking into these shanty towns. There was a day when he was ranching when every month the banker from town would ride out and leave the hands' payroll in a canvas bag on a boulder on the edge of the range to save him a forty-mile round trip to the Wild Rose ranch-house. It might sit there for days and no man would dream of touching it, except perhaps some passing Comanche, who wouldn't have much use for it either. Even Murchison's riff-raff, skunks as they

---

[1]Muggers

were, wouldn't stoop so low. "Now," he came to the conclusion, "anything goes. Purty soon I'll have to trail a lariat into the saloon to hang onto my hoss while I'm wetting my whistle."

And talking about lowdown polecats here came another. Young Lucifer Grattan himself, swaggering into the saloon, Big Jake close on his heels. He slapped the boy called Billy Joe on the back. As Billy Joe stepped back to make room at the bar, Big Jake stuck his foot out and sent him sprawling. His head clopped like a coconut on the floorboards.

The boy picked himself up, charged into Jake, waving a forefinger in his face. "I'm a patient person, but one of these days I'm gonna snap. I'm gonna settle with you, you big ape."

Jake grinned his little bad and blackened teeth, and hammered a fist down on the kid's head, squashing his bowler over his eyes. "Oh yeah?"

The boy went bow-legged, dazed and spinning, half-blinded by his hat, groping for the day. Jake helped him on his way out of the saloon with a boot up his backside and giggled. He was having a great day. "He'll have a sore head tomorrow and it won't just be the whiskey. Maybe he'll remember Big Jake."

Pete recalled the leer on Jake's face as he helped the *bandidos* tread the clouds. There was a man who enjoyed hurting and humiliating people. The funeral director's best friend.

Lucifer Grattan had spotted Pete and strolled over to offer his hand. "Howdy. You new in town?"

"Guess I must be or you wouldn't ask," Pete growled, ignoring the hand.

Nonetheless, Lucifer sat in a chair across from him, his poisonous eyes flickering on the silver-eagle revolvers on Pete's belt. "Nice pair of firearms. May I take a look?"

"Nobody touches my guns 'cept me." Pete filled his glass from the bottle, not inviting Grattan to join him. "Ain't you the executioner?"

"Yeh, great necktie party, huh? I organised the whole thing."

"Ever thought one day somebody might be doin' that to you?"

"No." Grattan started at the fierceness of the black-bearded man's regard. "Nobody'll do that to me. I'll die with a gun in my hand."

"Maybe sooner than you think."

Pete's words hung like a menace in the suddenly quiet saloon. "Ain't you the punk who's set hisself up as sheriff of this town?"

"What if I am?" Lucifer said, his hand going towards his Magnum, his fingers flickering on the butt, unsure of himself, of the other man. "You lookin' for me?"

"Nope." Pete smiled without warmth in his eyes. "Jest checkin' if what I hear is correct. That you're the greasiest lil rat this side of the Colorado River. I reckon that must be the truth."

Lucifer gave a gasping laugh, his buck teeth grinning, his cheek dimpling. He was one of those villains not without a boyish charm. "I reckon you heard right. What I want to know is which trail you took into this town?"

"I came along the trail from Santa Fe. Why?"

"You didn't come across from south New Mexico through the red canyons? You didn't cross Rioja's land yesterday?"

"I told you which way I come from. Ain't never been to south New Mexico."

"Where you from then?" Lucifer pressed.

"You sure are a nosey lil gopher, aincha? Guess it's this idea you've got that you're a lawman. Tell you what, brother, one of these days soon enough this territory's goin' to get statehood and they'll be installing some properly appointed marshals. Whatcha goin' do then?"

"That's when you and me both will be headin' for the border," Grattan grinned. "No, come on, I'm only bein' friendly. What's your name? Where you from?"

"I don't have no name. I find it's the best policy. If you need to, you can call me Missouri. That's where I hail from," Pete lied. "That's where I fought in the war under the black flag. Since then I've drifted through the Kansas cowtowns, Dodge, Abilene, Newton. Seems like I allus got to keep movin' on. Did some huntin' in Injin Territory 'fore I headed down here. That satisfy you?"

"What sort of huntin'?"

"Man-huntin'. For bounty. You heard of the Doolin gang? I killed three of 'em."

"Yeah? I heard somebody had got them boys."

Lucifer's look of shifty suspicion began to change to one of a certain awe. "If you fought under the black flag you must know the James boys."

Pete lit a cheroot and tipped the bottle again. This little cuss took some lying to. Although he had never actually met the world's two most famous outlaws, he grimaced and

110

said, "Those are two men if you know anything about you don't mention it to nobody. They're liable to turn up on your doorstep."

"Ha!" Lucifer Grattan said, as if absorbing all this. "Well, if you're half the man you reckon you are, maybe I could use you. Interested?"

"At the moment," Pete drawled, blowing his smoke into the youth's thin spotty face, "I happen to be on the trail of a blue-eyed chickadee called Lil Moll. She double-crossed the Doolins and got away with a fortune in gold ingots. You ain't seen her by any chance?"

"No," Lucifer said, puzzled. "Nevuh heard of her."

"Guess she's south of the line by now."

"Well? I'm gettin' short of men. This Rioja man I told you about has got hisself some kinda shootist. He killed seven of my boys yesterday."

"Mebbe I can help out," Pete mused. "I charge 50 dollars per job, payment by silver. In advance."

"Fifty dollars! Nobody gets that much."

"I do."

"OK. I'll have to confirm it with the boss."

"Who's he?"

"Buddy, that's something *I* don't even know. Nor, come to that, do I really know anything about you. I don't even know if you can shoot."

"See that fly on that pretty gal's head?" Pete whipped out his left-hip silver-eagle Frontier, stretched out his arm. 'Ker-*ASH*!' — the weapon karoomed, and the silver wig on Esmeralda, busy chattering on the far side of the saloon, was whipped away to show her round skull of black curls. "It ain' there no more."

Esmeralda screamed and clutched her bare head.

"What in hail? What's happenin'? Gee-sus, Fingal, cain't yo' *do* somethun'? A lady ain' safe in here."

The men around her laughed, with

something akin to relief, as they saw the dark stranger holster his revolver.

"You're in. Fifty an outing," Lucifer quickly agreed. "Now, here's the layout. Rioja runs a spread fifteen miles outa town. We want that land."

"Why?"

"That's none of your business. All you have to help do is run off his lousy gutless greasers."

"It wouldn't be that somebody reckons there's a seam of silver on that land?"

"How did you know?"

"Pretty obvious. You wouldn't be goin' to all this trouble to herd a few cows."

"You're right." Lucifer lowered his voice. "Our surveyor is certain there's a seam running from Henry Higgins' mine out through the range of hills and surfacing on Rioja's land."

"Maybe I should put my price up," Pete said.

"Look, this is an easy job. There's only the old man and a few of his

113

vaqueros left. I've already killed his son."

"You have?"

"Yeah. Well, he asked for it. Came looking for me. Luckily I was ready for him" — Lucifer gave a cunning smile — "I had Big Jake up in the livery loft with a rifle. As Raoul drew he shot him in the back."

"Yeah?"

"Yeah. I'm not one for all this gentlemanly man to man duelling. That's for fools and corpses. The stuff of dime novels. It makes me sick."

"You've got a point. That's how many a good man's got hisself dead. It's allus best to have the edge."

Lucifer looked behind him as a commotion broke out in the bar. A big lumberjack-type, a permanent grin on his ugly mug, was trying to grope Esmeralda and refusing to pay Fingal's dues. He was getting a trifle nasty. He had already smashed a beer glass into the face of one man who tried to intervene, and was currently tossing another across the bar.

"Aw, Jeez! That guy makes me sick, too. This is the third time I've warned him."

Before anybody could say Bob's your uncle a long lovingly-honed kitchen knife appeared in Lucifer's fingers, and he slung it full force through the gawping heads to embed in the lumberjack's back. The man groaned and thudded forwards to the boards, his hands grasping vainly for the weapon. He kicked and twitched and choked like some gutted fish as his check shirt was blotted with blood and he slowly expired.

Lucifer went across, put his foot on his back, hefted the knife out, wiped the blade on his pants and said, "Get this stiff outa here."

"Now I know why they call you El Cuchillo," Pete said when he returned.

"Yeah. Not a bad throw, eh? It's good to have a real target for a change. Kinda more satisfyin'." El Cuchillo grinned, hungrily, adjusting his blue bandanna and taking a leather pouch from the pocket of his black leather waistcoat, tossing it to Pete. "There's fifty dollars of silver. Weigh it if you like. We ride at dawn."

"Where to?"

"River Bend. There ain't gonna be no gunplay. We're short-handed and I'm not sure about that new man they've got. We've hired some army sappers from Fort Apache. For a small remuneration they are gonna dam the Rio Diablo just at the point before it enters Miguel del Rioja's land. They are gonna turn it in a different direction. He's gonna have some thirsty cows. That land will be useless to him without water. He will have to get out."

"Can they do that?" Pete was genuinely surprised. Not that anybody could be so treacherous, but that army personnel were getting involved.

"Of course they can. They will be using dynamite, the latest equipment. And we own the land on this side of his line. Why shouldn't we change the

116

course of our river? It's all perfectly legal. That's the beauty of the idea. I tell you the man I take my orders from is no lame-brain."

"Nope," — Pete shook his head with awe, the Rioja family had been using that water for a hundred years and now it would be taken away from them at a stroke — "He certainly ain't. Whoever he is."

Pete picked up the silver and tucked it in his shirt pocket as Esmeralda minced over in her tight silver dress. "Lucifer," she called. "My hero! You rescued me. Thank the lawd you gave that big jerk his calling-card. He was becoming somewhat tiresome, poor dear." She slid her tight buttocks onto Pete's knee and coiled a brown braceleted arm around his neck. "And who's this tall dark handsome stranger who's been havin' games with me? Didja take a shot at me 'cause you wan' a shot at me? Ooh, what is this long hard thung ah'm sat upon?"

"That's my gun," Pete said, unable

to stifle a grin as he tried to fight her off.

"Are you sure?" Esmeralda grinned widely, her fingers getting everywhere.

Pete looked into her dark eyes which gleamed with mischief, recoiled from her overpowering perfume, held onto her slim wrists to try to restrain her. He squirmed to escape her, but he had to admit there was something enticing about this wriggling, giggling black pythoness, who was tickling and teasing and trying to poke her pink tongue between his lips. Or was it that he hadn't had a woman for over a year, keeping himself clean for Louisa (to what avail?). Suddenly he could understand why some men forgot themselves. No, enough was enough! He picked her up, strode to the swing doors and pitched her through them. She landed in a squawking heap on the sidewalk.

"I'd better find myself a decent gal pretty soon," he muttered. "Or I'll go crazy."

He looked around the establishment and met the goo-goo eyes of Double-barrelled Annie. "Hi," she called, fluttering her pudgy fingers.

"No *thank* you." He went out back to release some beer and was standing by the fence when Big Jake stumbled out and unbuttoned beside him. "I bet ya a quarter I can piss further than you," the idiot boasted, like some schoolboy.

"I ain't never tried pissing further than a skunk," Pete growled and moved away.

He strolled off to take a look at the town and muttered, "Jesus, what kinda dingbat's nest *is* this?"

9

AS soon as darkness fell Pete saddled his grey and slipped away from Diablo City, climbing past the campfires and devastated land of the mining-camps until he reached the side of the hill range that ran through the Rioja land. A fine excitement filled his soul as he hung over the horse's neck to avoid any low branches of the sweet-smelling *pinons* that girdled the hillsides. A thick cloud that had kept the early night as black as ink shifted and a three-quarters full moon appeared, seeming to sail through the drifting cumulii so that he could see below them the shelf of gleaming silver sage that stretched towards the *rancho*. He let the filly have her head for her eyes were better than his to see any unannounced obstacles as they went galloping through the night. He kept to the hills most of the way in case of any pursuit. When he heard the lowing of cattle and saw the red pinpoint of a *vaquero*'s cigarette as he rode watch around the herd, he set the filly charging nimble-footed down the mountainside, leaping fallen logs, and swerving around great boulders until he reached the valley bottom. He slowed the horse to a lope so as not to frighten the longhorns and rode towards the man, who was singing gently in soft Spanish to calm the beeves.

"*Aiyaiyee, hombre! Que pasa*," the man called, but recognized the horse gleaming white in the moonlight, and her rider, and beckoned them onwards.

The lookout opened the gate when he saw him coming and Pete was ushered into the Rioja's ranch-house. Juanita gave a gasp of surprise when she saw him, and her father cried out, "You are back soon. What's wrong?"

"Plenty," Pete said. "They are planning to dynamite your river. You've got to act fast."

He explained that whoever was backing El Cuchillo had somehow managed to get the army's help. The only thing to do was to ambush them while El Cuchillo's force was under strength.

"Try not to hit any army personnel. We don't want some kind of incident on our hands. I've a strong feeling this isn't a legitimate cavalry exercise. I reckon those sappers will be moonlighting and won't be expecting or wanting trouble."

Juanita pressed a cup of coffee on him, and he warmed himself, standing with his back to the fire. "And, another thing, try to capture their explosives. We may be able to use them. Tell your men to be careful where they're shooting with all that dynamite about."

"What about you?" Juanita asked.

"Yeah, I'd be mighty appreciative if you told your boys not to shoot at me or my horse. Take every man you've got and be in position well before sun-up."

"Maybe you should wear a white shirt to make you more distinctive," the girl suggested.

"Yeah, maybe this one could do with a wash," Pete grinned, as he pulled off his canvas one, and put on the one she gave him. "I'd better be getting back now."

"*Señor* Pete," the white-haired Mexican hidalgo cried as the cowboy jumped back on the grey. "Thank you."

"Don't thank me yet," Pete shouted, and whirled the filly around to send her at a fast lope back towards town.

★ ★ ★

It was still dark before dawn when El Cuchillo and his men rode out towards River Bend. There were about a dozen of them accompanying a detachment of six soldiers leading mules loaded with boxes of explosives. Black Pete was mightily relieved to see that there were so few soldiers. It reinforced his

123

notion that this was an unofficial expedition. The sergeant-in-charge was a scurvy-faced individual, narrow-eyed, muscular and sun-beaten in his faded blues and forage cap. He looked the sort who would be open to any bribe.

To reach River Bend they would have to pass through a narrow canyon of black basalt cliffs. On account of the mules they slowed their pace and splashed along through the river shallows. Once through the canyon the river turned towards the Rioja range and it was here that they planned to bring the cliffs crashing down to block its path.

The stars were dimming and morning beginning to lighten the sky as, harness creaking and spurs and bridles jingling, they clattered along. Only one man was not surprised as carbine and rifle fire cracked out from the cliffs on either side of them. But 'Missouri' acted as surprised as any of them as confusion reigned. He skittered his grey back and forth, aiming his new revolvers up at the cliffs, but making sure he fired high over the heads of those up there. El Cuchillo was screaming and cursing for one of the first bullets had got him in the thigh. Big Jake was roaring up that he would kill them all with his bare hands if they would only come down, his guns barking out as others of his comrades were pitched from their saddles. The soldiers had grim looks on their faces as they knelt down behind small boulders and tried to return fire. But the Mexicans were well-concealed and their fire withering. The gunshots went echoing, whining, whistling and booming between the canyon walls.

"We're getting out," the sergeant-in-charge shouted in panic. "Retreat, men."

At that point Pete decided to take a dive, throwing up his arms and tumbling from the grey. He lay face down, playing possum, as the hooves clattered about him and lead chipped the rocks. It took all of his nerve to stay that way when a nearby mule went up in an almighty explosion and he was showered with blood and guts and flying debris. The other terrified mules began braying and kicking and pulling away to go charging off along the canyon, as the survivors of this expedition of dam-busters backed away, until more fire made them turn tail and head their horses back in the direction they had come from as fast as they could go.

A rough tongue licked Pete's ear. The worried filly nudged and nuzzled the only man who had ever been kind to her. At first she had dashed off after the mules but had returned to look for him. He turned over and grinned up at her: "We fooled 'em, eh, babe?"

As the gunsmoke drifted away the Mexicans climbed down to take a look at the bodies, strip them of any valuables and finish off any who were wounded and writhing in agony.

"A good haul. Another eight of the rattlesnakes dead," Miguel del Rioja said, as he grinned down from beneath his big sombrero at Pete. "This is the second time you have saved us. I never thought I would owe so much to an *Americano*."

"Let's hope we are as lucky the third time," Pete said, and jumped back on the grey. "Because they ain't likely to give up."

10

IT was a sorry pack of scarred and whipped wolves who rode back to their lair in Diablo City. The sergeant and his sappers had trailed off to Fort Apache bemoaning the loss of their mules. "They dry-gulched us," Lucifer Grattan shouted as he limped into the Silver Nugget. "Some rat tipped them off."

"Who could that have been?" Fingal O'Rafferty tried to conceal the smirk on his fat face for he was much amused by their discomfiture. Suddenly the sheriff and his 'deputies' were not as cocky as was customary. "Here, boys, have a drink on the house," he said. "Drown your sorrows."

"Maybe it was that new man, what's his name, Missouri," Big Jake slurred. "Somethun' funny 'bout him."

"No." Lucifer winced as he rolled

up his trouser leg and examined the red hole in his thigh. It made him feel sick. Other people's blood never bothered him. But this was his own blood. This was different. "I saw him shot from his saddle. Lot of good he was. Fifty dollars I paid him."

"That ain' fair," Big Jake moaned. "You only paid me five."

"Arr, shuddup. You ain't even worth that. None of you are." El Cuchillo looked around at the remains of his gunmen who cringed under his gaze like beaten dogs. "You call yourselves hard men. You can't even sort out a few greasers. What am I gonna do about my leg?"

"That don't look too good, Mr Grattan," Fingal said, with a twinkle in his eye. "That certainly don't. You get gangrene, you could lose that leg."

Lucifer Grattan's Adam's apple visibly bobbed as he swallowed his alarm, a self-piteous note to his voice as he whined, "What am I gonna do?"

"I really don't know," Fingal said.

"I'm not so hot on first-aid and the doctor's out of town."

* * *

Billy Joe had chosen the biggest diamond ring in his pawnshop to put on Prissy's finger, made of rich yellow gold with two rubies on either side of the diamond. It must have been one the *bandidos* overlooked. Of course, it didn't cost him anything but he put a dollar in the till by way of keeping the books straight. He had bought a *garafon* jug of dago red, as El Cuchillo called it, and a bottle of real 'French Champagne' from Fingal to celebrate his engagement. He had invited Prissy to take a look at his surgery and persuaded her to take a sip of bubbly although she was an avowed enemy of demon drink.

"Come on, Prissy, just this once," he said. "It's a special occasion."

"Just this once," she murmured, as she arranged her somewhat heavy body in its rustling finery upon his creaking *chaise-longue* and quaffed a glass. "Mmm, it's rather nice. Well, perhaps just a little drop more."

"I'm gonna send to San Francisco for one of those drills. The latest state of the art. Foot-pump action, precision drilling. Means you can save the tooth 'stead of always yanking it out."

"You're so ambitious," Prissy said, proudly, as she picked bits of lint off his suit.

Billy Joe took a swig of the jug to give him courage. The sight of Prissy's white-stockinged ankle had inflamed him. He dived his hand under her skirts — how many durned petticoats had she? — and groped for her knee. "Billy!" she cried, going rigid as he tried to kiss her and his nose plunged down into her sweetsmelling neckline to explore her massive mammaries. "How dare you?"

"But we're engaged," he protested, his arms encircling her, looking up, desperately, into her blue orbs.

"That doesn't mean you can take familiarities." But she smiled sweetly down at him, giggling as the bubbly got up her nose. She patted his head to her bosom. "There, my little dove, nestle there."

He lay upon her, swaddled in her arms, and patted like a little pet dog. But there was no fun in that, so he took another swig of the vile red and attacked again.

"Billy!" she shouted, as if he were a naughty boy in her class, as his fingers managed to unbutton her blouse and he glimpsed the heave of white pneumatic flesh at last. She gave him a shove and he landed with a crash on the floorboards. "I expect you to respect me."

"Forgive me," he groaned, kissing her ankles, poking his head up beneath her crinolines, kissing all the way up to her thighs. "It's just that I want you so," he muttered, lost in her skirts.

Prissy gave a shriek, although pausing a few moments, breathless at this strange sensation between her legs, before she pushed him away. "What sort of girl do you think I am?"

"That's what I want to find out," he slurred. But by then Billy Joe was too drunk to know what he was up to, toppling backwards over his gas canisters. Prissy demanded to be taken home and he weaved along beside her, hiccuping and apologising, back to the white house.

"Silly Billy," she said, kissing his lips. "I think the sooner we are married the better it will be. Go back to bed now like a good boy."

Billy Joe finished off the two-gallon jug when he got back, and sprawled out on his *chaise-longue*. The heady wine gave him all kinds of strange thoughts that his brain would never have harboured before. Did he want to get married? Wasn't he, as Fingal said, too young? She was, after all, much older than him. Why couldn't she . . . just . . .

As lurid imaginations of what might

occur filled his brain his eye alighted on his laughing-gas. An evil idea occurred to him, appalling in its effrontery. Why not, next time, give her a whiff? Put her under his power? Then he would find out what a naked woman was like without her knowing anything about it!

Yes! Brilliant! He put the mask on himself for a quick gulp. And fell asleep laughing hilariously at his ingenious plot.

★ ★ ★

"What's up, doc?" Fingal asked, as Billy Joe pushed through the batwing doors in the early morning. "You look like you could do with a hair of the dog. How did your courting go?"

Billy Joe gave a grimace. "I don't rightly recall. Give me a whiskey and soda. I do believe I'm in the doghouse."

"For a boy who took his first drink two days ago you've certainly shown an uncanny appreciation of the gladsome

134

grog," Fingal said, filling a tumbler and watching the tousled youth push his bowler to the back of his head and down it in one.

Billy Joe looked about him and saw El Cuchillo and his disconsolate band. "Hi! You boys been in the wars?"

El Cuchillo eyed him venomously, as if he would just as soon put his knife into this tenderfoot's chest. His thin, long-nosed face was even more pale than usual, his slit of lips set grimly as if in pain. Behind him hovered the great ugly giant, Jake, who rarely left his side.

"He got a Minie ball through his thigh," Jake growled.

"Damblasted sawbones is outa town," Lucifer said. "Can't get no treatment. Say, you gotta surgery, aincha? Know anything about doctoring?"

"Me?" Billy Joe met the green glimmering eyes, startled, but somehow excited by El Cuchillo's regard. "I've got disinfectant and stuff. I could clean it up for you."

"You reckon so?"

"Sure." It felt good for once to be taken seriously by these outlaws. Suddenly an urge came over him to be like them. Miss Prissy was all very well with her goody-goodiness. But he wanted to be bad. He was sick of being a sissy. He wanted to be a *man*. "If I do that for you, Mistuh Grattan, what will you do for me?"

"Whatja mean?" El Cuchillo laughed in his sarcastic manner. "Whadja want me to do?"

"Teach me how to use a gun and a knife like you do."

"Hey! The boy wants to be a badman. You'd better not drink any more if you're goin' to operate on me." He reached out an arm and squeezed Billy Joe to him. "OK. It's a deal. Lead on."

"What's goin' on?" Esmeralda shrilled as she clattered down on high heels from the bedrooms, a purple ostrich-feather-trimmed gown wrapped around her skinny body. "Cain't a gal get any

136

sleep? Oh, I say, you two look like you're gettin' mighty friendly."

Big Jake looked anxious. "You ain't lettin' this milk-sop ride with us?"

"Sho. You stay here. Me an' Billy Joe's got business."

He hobbled out of the doors, hanging onto the boy's shoulders.

"Well, fiddle-de-dee, whatever next!" Esmeralda grimaced as she looked into the mirror. "Oh, my gawd. I need to put my face on. The things a gal has to do. And I must get a new wig. That stranger ruined mine."

"I don't trust that lil runt," Big Jake said. "There's somethun' funny about him."

"Ah, sweetie," Esmeralda cooed. "Has he taken your leader from you? You big bad boys will be the death of me."

Over the street, as Billy Joe helped El Cuchillo up to his surgery he felt a strange thrill of collusion with the young killer. He sat him down on the *chaise-longue* and said, "Let me take

137

a look." He knelt down and scissored away the trousers from the wound. He undid the greasy bandanna, sticky with blood, to reveal a ragged red hole in the thigh flesh. He began dabbing at it and El Cuchillo gave a scream. So he wasn't as brave as he pretended to be? "Sorry," he said. "Maybe I should give you a whiff of gas? Slug's gone right through the flesh. Don't seem to have caught the bone. Got to get any dirt out."

He looked up into the killer's cat-green eyes, and for moments it seemed as if a challenge passed between them. He twitched his nostrils, for a feral smell seemed to emanate from El Cuchillo, the smell of a wild animal. "Sure, kid," Grattan nodded. "Anything you say."

He closed the mouthpiece over El Cuchillo's face and watched him as he began to giggle. How relaxed his usually tense face had become! Eyes closed, he looked almost boyishly innocent. And the nitrous oxide was beginning to have its strange side-effect. What a thin line there was between good and evil. How easy to step over.

Billy Joe worked quickly, expertly, bandaging the wound. The gunslinger was well away. Billy stood, smiled, and tousled the youth's black hair, a familiarity El Cuchillo would certainly not have allowed him. In spite of the killer's coldness and cruelties Billy Joe had a fondness for him. As if he might be some demonic brother, the other side of his own personality, a person he, himself, might easily have become if he had not had such a decent upbringing. He shuddered as he looked down at him and whispered, "You are my evil twin."

He held his breath, and slipped the big Magnum .357 out of El Cuchillo's holster. He raised it to aim at the youth's forehead. It was so heavy he could hardly hold it without wavering. He could kill him now and it would be all over. There was probably a big reward on him. El Cuchillo's terrorizing of innocents would be at an end.

Billy Joe forced himself to move the gun away, and as he did so his finger squeezed the trigger, and it kicked as it exploded, knocking him backwards, the bullet shattering the window.

Lucifer Grattan flickered his eyes open. "What 'n hell you doin', Billy Joe?"

"Nothing," the boy said, recovering himself. "It went off. I was just trying it."

"You wanna be careful, boy." Grattan passed his hand over his eyes, groggily. "Jeez, funny dreams I had. Dreamed somebody was gonna kill me."

Billy Joe gave the flicker of a smile. "Come," he said, helping him up. "You promised to show me."

★ ★ ★

The beer bottles balanced on the fence smashed to smithereens — one, two, three, four — as the gun in Billy Joe's hands roared.

"Jee-sus! Four outa five. Set 'em up again, Billy Joe. You're a natural. I nevuh seen shootin' like it for a first-timer. You sure about that?"

"Yes. This is the first time. I find this gun much easier." He reloaded the Remington Storekeeper .38 with a three and a half inch barrel which he had found in his pawnshop. A much neater, lighter weapon than the Magnum, it could easily be carried in a pocket or tucked in his belt. It held five bullets. He felt excited, as if suddenly he was somebody to be reckoned with. He had the power of life or death in his hand. It was like being God.

"The boy's showing the same aptitude for shootin' as he has for drinkin'," Fingal said, with awe. He had come out with Esmeralda and some of the boys into the backyard to watch. "A little more practice and he'll be a crack shot."

141

Billy Joe stood, narrowed his eyes, whipped the Remington from his belt, and fired again, sweeping the weapon along, not needing to cock it with his thumb, for it was a double-action, concentrating hard. And grinned as every bottle in the line went down.

"What you need to do now is kill a man," El Cuchillo laughed, hobbling over to him. "To get the feel of what that thing's really made for."

Billy Joe looked at the jeering youth, at the gun in his hand, with dismay. Could he ever do that? He licked his lips with fear and excitement. Did he want to?

Lucifer Grattan squeezed the boy's shoulder. "We could do with somebody who knows doctoring ridin' with us. What say you, boys? Shall we let him join the gang?"

Billy Joe felt embarrassed, uneasy. "I don't know," he stuttered. What about Prissy? His parents? What would they say? He knew they would be horrified. "I . . . I'm a professional man. Just need something to defend myself."

But, as he stood there with El Cuchillo's hand on his shoulder, he felt as if the killer had some strange power over him.

11

"**THEM** Diablo scum won't dare attack until they've recruited some more gunslingers. We've put 'em outa business for a while. What I figure you should do, sir, is take this opportunity to light out for Tucson and find yourself some more *vaqueros*. There's a strong Mexican community there."

Black Pete was cleaning his silver enscrolled revolvers, taking them apart with a screwdriver, squinting along the barrels. He sat at the table on a horn and hide chair and imparted this advice to del Rioja, glancing across at him through the flickering candlelight. "If I were you I'd take your two best men as guards and bypass Diablo by night so nobody gets any fool ideas about following you. We oughta be safe here for a while."

The *haciendado* brushed a strong bronzed hand through his leonine head of white hair. "*Si, manana por el manana.*"[1]

"If you don't mind me suggestin', you mebbe oughta leave tonight. The sooner you're back the better. These bustards ain't gonna be long before they attack in force."

Miguel del Rioja's dark eyes searched his face as if for moments suspecting the gringo maybe had some ulterior motive, like robbing him, or raping his daughter. He was only a killer on the run, after all. But he pushed the thoughts away as foolish and said, "I think you are right. I will start immediately."

He jumped to his feet calling to the Opata squaw to pack him some meat jerky and hard biscuits, and went to look for his men.

---

[1]Tomorrow afternoon

145

"What's happening?" Juanita asked, as she came in carrying a jug of coffee.

"Your father's going to Tucson on business. If he's gonna hang onto this place he's badly in need of more men."

"*Si*. What will you do?"

He looked across at her, her slim waist in the loose skirt, the upward reach of her nubile diaphragm, the firm breasts pressing out her white blouse, her long neck and beautiful face. In the candlelight her eyes were the colour of a moonlit Mexican sky, deep purple in their intensity as she stared at him, with a touch of sadness tonight. "I reckon I'll find plenty to occupy me here."

She gave a slight smile, as if relieved that he was not going, too, and at the same time her cheeks coloured up and she quickly returned to her coffee-pouring, perhaps ashamed or startled by what had passed through her mind.

Mebbe I oughta go with him at

146

that, Pete thought. Be outa the way of temptation.

Whenever the girl was close to him it was as if an electrical current passed through his body drawing him to her and he knew, as it was impossible not to know, that something similar was going on inside her. He gritted his teeth and concentrated on putting the revolvers back together. He had no intention of taking advantage of one so young in her father's absence.

"Juanita," he drawled, slowly, because he liked the sound of her name.

"Si?" She looked up, apprehensively.

"Would you have any goose-fat in the house?"

"Yes, there is a bowl of it in the kitchen. Why?"

"I wanna grease my bullets. I'll get it."

Pete jumped up, but so did Juanita, and for moments they stood there. He put his long fingers out and gently clasped her waist, and the girl's heart pounded as she stared into his dark

147

visage. The sound of her father's voice in the hall made her break free, and she bounded away. "I know where it is," she called.

Miguel del Rioja strode in followed by two of his *charros* who carried rifles and belts of ammunition. He selected a Winchester carbine from the rack on the wall and swung a heavy striped serape over his shoulders.

"I bin thinkin'," Pete said. "Mebbe in Tucson it might be a good idea to renew your title to this land. And put an advertisement in the newspaper to say so."

"Why? This is my land. Everybody knows so."

"But there ain't nuthin' like havin' everything legal. My guess is your deeds go back to before the war between our two countries when your heroic Santa Anna handed everything over piecemeal."

"Yes, they do. I see what you mean."

"And it might make sense to go see the governor, tell him what's going on, and see if he can't do anything. Only you'll need to take a bag of silver with you. Slip it across his desk."

"A *mordida*? The governor?"

"Sure, that's the way we gringos go on. Nobody does nobody no favours for nuthin' out here."

"I am an honourable man, *señor*. I cannot do that."

"Suit yourself, Miguel. One more request. I fancy doin' a bit of prospecting on your land. In partnership with you, of course. So why not make out a claim? That'd stop any other galoot from thinkin' he can come nosin' about around here."

"You mean you think there might be something worth mining for?"

Pete nodded his head in assent. "Not only me. Others are thinking it, too. Whadja think this whole war's about? It ain't jest range rights."

"I see." Del Rioja tugged at his long moustaches, thoughtfully.

"Must you go so suddenly, father?" Juanita had returned from the kitchen with the goose-grease.

"Yes. Our young American friend has convinced me. Be kind to him while I am gone."

"Oh, I will. Can't you see I am already running his errands for him?" and Juanita laughed as she followed the men out to say goodbye.

Pete was finishing his coffee when she returned, and watched her as she busied herself at the hearth of the big stone fireplace.

"I will make a fire. It gets chilly at night here on the high chapparal. And it is more cheerful, too."

When she had got a blaze going they drew their chairs up and stared into the flames. Now that they were suddenly alone, for the Opata woman had gone off duty to the cabin where she lived with her children, an ominous silence seemed to fall over them. It was as if both knew what the other was thinking but neither would be the first to speak.

Finally Pete muttered, "I ain't used

to sleepin' indoors on soft beds. For the past two months I been mainly sleepin' out under the stars. I guess I'll take my blanket out onto the veranda."

As he got to his feet, Juanita called out, "Don't." She knelt down on the bearskin rug and shook her dark hair down over her shoulders. "Don't leave me, Pete."

He stared at her for a few moments and shook his head. "It ain't right. You're only a girl. Your father's just walked out the house. He trusts me."

Juanita slowly undid the buttons of her blouse and pulled it apart to reveal her naked body. "That was foolish of him, wasn't it?"

"I told you, I . . . I'm a no-good outlaw . . . on the dodge. What do you — ?"

"Do I have to beg you?" The girl's eyes were vividly violet in their intensity in the dancing flames. "Must I abandon all pride?"

"Aw, hell," Pete said, tossing his hat aside.

He knelt down beside her, placed his large hands with awe on her pale and wondrously moulded breasts, squeezing them together, stooping to kiss her pink uptilted nipples.

Juanita stroked her hands through his dark shaggy hair and closed her eyes with pleasure. "Teach me to be a woman," she whispered.

"It's been so long I'd almost forgotten what a gal feels like," he said, and pressed her gently back onto the fur.

"What does she feel like?"

"Damn wonderful. Worth waiting for," he said, as he kissed her.

12

BILLY JOE'S courtship of Prissy was not proving successful — to his way of thinking — although he had managed to persuade her to return to his surgery, and even to enter the little back bedroom and recline on the iron brass-knobbed bed (in which the pawnbroker had been savagely beaten to death). But she had refused to go under the gas. Funnily enough, her ardour was equal to his. They would kiss and cuddle until their lips were sore. But somehow he was no nearer to his target, that's to say to getting his hands on those portions of her anatomy that he was not meant to. Indeed, Billy Joe found Miss Prissy's attack somewhat overpowering. Their grappling had come to resemble a wrestling-match. Whenever his prying fingers approached the goal the schoolmistress would squeal like a stuck pig, and as if at a bell signifying the end of a bout would hurl him out of the ring, or bed, to land with a bang on the floor.

"Billy Joe," she would chide him. "I never dreamed you were such a naughty boy."

He would climb back to her and begin the process all over again — round two! — or maybe three or four — until finally she would announce it was time for her to go. And he would see her back to the Rev Spank's presbytery. He hated going into the parlour there for the clergyman was apt to stare at him in an accusatory way, or try to play footsie under the table again. There was something very creepy about the reverend. Hot and flustered, Billy Joe would hurry away and generally find solace in the rough companionship in the Silver Nugget and in a bottle of red-eye. He had developed a stupendous thirst and would weave back to his surgery in a stupor. Surely this was why so many crimes occurred in this territory — from sheer drunkenness and sexual frustration.

However, when he counted up his receipts at the end of the week Billy Joe realized that he was doing well. In line with the inflationary practices of a bonanza town he was charging sky-high, fifty cents an extraction. And they were queueing at his surgery door. Maybe some simply wanted to see what the effects of laughing-gas were like. Others must have been going round with inflamed gums for years. He sold them his new bristle toothbrushes and advised them to always carry one in a pocket. If a client claimed he couldn't pay Billy Joe accepted whatever he had to offer in kind, like a shovel or watch. He even accepted a cow-horse from some galoot, and the scrubby Appaloosa now awaited his pleasure in the livery. Running up and down between the pawnshop and the surgery was proving tiresome. He might have to get a man in to mind the store. But he reckoned he could prove himself to his father to be a successful businessman.

Although he had not yet been able to entice Prissy to go under the gas, he was working on her. But would he, he wondered, have the courage when it came to the crunch to have his wicked way with her? It was something that occupied his mind. He had tried to convince her of his honourable intentions and his devotion to religion. He took her to the Spanish mission church where old Mexican women huddled in their mantillas counting their beads before the great altar of the cruelly crucified Christ.

Prissy was upset by the service. "Why does the priest have to speak in Latin? I couldn't understand a word. Why must they wallow in the blood and thorns? In my church we talk about Jesus welcoming little children and all the good things he does. I don't think I could ever convert to Roman Catholic ways. I would so miss our lovely plain prayers and hymns."

Yuk, he thought, and would go and get drunk and practise his shooting. How satisfying it was to smash a few bottles. When he got hungry he would wander along to the reverend's house because he was very fond of Prissy's molasses biscuits. He would stand and watch her kneeding dough, flour on her pudgy nose, dimples in her elbows, in her mob-cap and pinafore. Could a man be in love with a woman for her cooking skills, he wondered?

"I do declare we only see the boy at mealtimes," the Rev Ebediah Spank remarked as they sat down to a dinner of pork chops and boiled cabbage. "And far too often his breath stinks of whiskey. *Acutus descensus avernii*. Steep is the slippery slope into Hell. Dante's Inferno. Repent, Billy Joe, before it is too late. Remember Proverbs 20: 'Wine is a mocker. And whosoever is deceived thereby is not wise'."

"Have you heard from your parents yet?" Miss Prissy put in. "It would be nice to have their blessing. Perhaps we could go to San Francisco for the nuptials?"

"No, not yet" — it was an honest reply for Billy Joe had not yet written to them — "I don't want to go home. I like it out here."

"Ah, but you'll be needing a financial settlement when you're man and wife," the minister said.

"I can manage without 'em."

"Don't speak with your mouth full, Billy Joe." Prissy chided. "What kind of attitude is that?"

"Yes, I would have thought they would at least send a substantial money-order so the happy young couple could set themselves up in a decent house," the Rev Spank said. "You might have a little addition to the family one day. For man is born to cleave unto woman."

"Maybe you should mind your own business," Billy Joe snapped.

"Billy Joe! How dare you speak to a man of the cloth like that?"

"I'll speak to him anyways I like."

"My, what a surly boy you are. Apologize to the reverend this instant. This is his house we're in."

"I surely won't. I've told you I'm going to make my own way in life. I don't want to go begging on Mama and Dad."

An indignant silence hung over the table for the rest of the meal. Billy Joe tried to appease Prissy by washing the dishes. When he went into the scullery Miss Prissy was sat embroidering a sampler with the motto, 'Rest Thy Burden Upon the Lord'. Yes, he wished he could. He watched her needle going deftly in and out, heard her gingham dress and petticoats creaking starchily. There was a furrowed frown between her eyebrows. Something formidable about Prissy.

"Are you coming to the surgery tonight?" he ventured.

"No, I'm not," she said. "I don't like your behaviour. It's not gentlemanly."

"Hot damn," Billy Joe shouted. "I'm going for a beer."

"I told you the devil's in that boy," the Rev Spank shouted as Billy Joe crashed out of the door. "He shall come to destruction."

I can't stand it any more, he thought, as he hurried away. She's driving me crazy.

Sometimes, it seemed, he preferred the evil El Cuchillo's company to hers, the coarse jokes of his hired guns to her innocuous chatter. The only one he couldn't bear was Big Jake who was forever burping his foul breath in his face, calling him half-pint, or playing tricks on him.

That night, because of the argument with Prissy, he wasn't properly concentrating on what he was doing. He had decided not to drink too much and to go back and apologize to her. He picked up his bowler hat, and put it on and — eugh! — it had been filled with molasses by Big Jake. The revolting sticky substance ran through

160

his hair and down his face.

He vowed revenge. And the next day his chance occurred. Jake was nursing a swollen jaw. He had a bad case of pyorrhoea. He needed at least three big ones pulled. What a mess his mouth was. "Go on," Lucifer urged him. "The doc'll treat you. He'll put you asleep. You won't feel a thing."

Jake reluctantly went with him to the surgery. As the great-gutted cretin lolled there on the *chaise-longue* a wicked gleam came into the young dentist's eyes. It was certainly a struggle but he managed to yank out every one of Jake's teeth. There! Serve him right!

He strolled back over to the saloon before Jake had emerged from the effects of the gas. He was on his second glass of whiskey when the giant staggered through the swing doors, his gaping mouth a bloody hole.

"Look what he's done," he gabbled, almost in tears, and as the men began to laugh at his comical way of talking, Jake pulled his revolver and roared,

"I'm goin' a kill him."

Billy Joe froze as the revolver's deadly eye covered him. Flame and smoke bellowed and a bullet splintered the bar by his side. Jake was swaying unsteadily, still under the effects of the gas. But that was close. He was aiming the revolver again.

"Draw!" Lucifer shouted at the boy. "KILL HIM! You've got to."

A second bullet crashed bottles behind his head, singeing his cheek as Billy Joe stood there. But still he didn't move. The smoking revolver was pointing at him again, a hideous snarl on its owner's face.

"Kill him!" El Cuchillo screamed.

And as if in a trance Billy Joe took his Storekeeper from his waistband, stretched out his arm and emptied five bullets into Big Jake's guts. The giant went down leaking blood.

"Did you see that?" a man said. "As cool as a cucumber, the kid was."

Billy Joe looked down on the dead Jake lying in a widening pool of blood.

162

He felt as much pity for him as he might for some cockroach he had squashed. He resumed quaffing his whiskey, and lit himself a cheroot.

"That was great, Billy boy," El Cuchillo said, slapping him on the back. "You've the makings of a real shootist."

"He asked for it," Billy Joe said.

He stood there, the gun in his hand, stunned by a mixture of euphoria and dread. Was this what it was like to be a killer?

13

"I NEVER thought to see a boy like you turn killer," Fingal mused as he leaned his elbows on the bar and studied the corpse of Big Jake. "You'll have to clean up that mess, Billy Joe. He's leaking like a colander. I'm sick of scrubbing blood off my floorboards."

"That makes seventeen," El Cuchillo said, morosely. "Seventeen of my men given their tickets to the nether regions within a week. I hate to think what the Boss is goin' to say. Guess I'd better head for Silver City and rustle up some more *renegados*. If I'm gonna fight Rioja and his new man I badly need some gun-fodder."

He snapped his bullwhip out to teasingly nip at the hindquarters of Annie who sat on a bench, her eyes fixed catatonically on the bleeding body.

"That was a terrible thing to do, though, Billy Joe. I know he was a pig, but pulling all the teeth outa the poor man. Such a torment. You surely *made* him draw on you. It can't do your business any good whatever. Folks will be terrified of going to you."

"They *are* already," Billy Joe replied. "But mine is one of those secure professions, like an undertakers. Scared or not they always have to come to us in the end."

"Thou shalt not kill," the Reverend Ebediah Spank bellowed as he pushed into the saloon, Miss Prissy treading on his heels, her blue eyes saucers of indignation. "Will you disobey the Lord's commandments?" He stood and pointed an accusatory finger at the boy.

"We have heard. The whole town's heard. How can I marry you now?" Miss Prissy whined. "How could you do this to me, Billy Joe? The disgrace! The humiliation!"

"Gee, Prissy! He took two shots at

me. Durn near killed me. What else could I do?"

"'There is an evil which I have seen under the sun and it is common among men' — Ecclesiastes Six," the reverend intoned, holding aloft his good book.

"Awe, piss off, preacher," Double-barrelled Annie said, hardly stifling a yawn. "Go thump your bible somewhere else."

"And the dogs in the street shall eat Jezebel," Ebediah whinnied, his mane tossing, rearing up haughtily, pointing at the prostitute.

Double-barrelled Annie lit a cigarette, her reams of flesh struggling to escape from a tight scarlet shimmy, and her cupid painted lips pursed in a look of utter depravity — Fingal had considered sacking her but there was no accounting for men's tastes. She blew out the smoke and drawled, "Sure, and 'Ahab pisseth aginst the wall'! My ole man was another dumb bible toter."

"Hey! Howdee!" A gnarled prospector

who had slept through all the fighting woke from his alcoholic torpor and squeezed Miss Prissy's *derriere*. "We got a real good-lookin' gal here at last?"

Miss Prissy screamed and grabbed herself into the Rev Spank's side for protection. "Mercy! Such sinners. How can you defile yourself in such an establishment, Billy Joe."

A hideous hyena giggle came from the stairs down which Esmeralda was making her entrance. "Wha, don' tell me this is the lump of lard Billy Joe's bin bumpin'?" She made her way swaying sinuously down in her tight silver dress and purple boa. "Wha, I bet ah could give him a better time than you, teacher gal."

"Come away, Billy Joe," Miss Prissy pleaded, pulling the preacher back out of this place of sin. "Look at that poor soul's body there. Have you no shame?"

"The foolishness of man perverteth his ways," the reverend said. "Proverbs."

"*You* can talk about perverteth," Billy Joe said. "I know you. I'm going to Silver City with Lucifer. And you can't stop me. I'm tired of being preached at. You get on my nerves, both of you. That man" — he pointed at the bloody corpse and raised his voice — "got on my nerves. Anybody else gets on my nerves they're going to get the same treatment. Understand?"

"Billy! Don't! What's come over you?"

Miss Prissy tried to surge forward past the preacher but he held her back. "Stay, Miss Prissy. Let us leave this polluted place. Let us return to our church. 'For the name of the Lord is a strong tower. The righteous runneth into it and is safe'."

"Arr, clear off," Double-barrelled Annie howled, hurling expletives too uncouth for this narrative.

"Give me three fingers of red-eye," Billy Joe said, proudly, to Fingal. "I'm riding with El Cuchillo."

14

BLACK PETE awoke in a big four-poster oak bed entwined in the warm, soft, naked limbs of a young woman. "Where am I?" he wondered. "Am I dead and gone to paradise? No, that ain't likely, not with all the men I killed."

"They must have been bad men," Juanita's voice whispered in his ear. "So the Lord will forgive you."

"Well, mostly it was them or me." He turned and met her eyes vividly violet in the morning sunshine that streaked through the bars of the bedroom window, felt her lips, soft as petals, brush his face, and realized that he, too, was naked beneath the sheet. "Whadda ya know!"

"I believe in the God of vengeance. A man cannot turn the other cheek. Not in this wild country."

"Nope. He can barely chance to turn his back. I learned that sure enough down at the Wild Rose." A frown paused over his saturnine features as the memories stabbed into him and he struggled up. "The law of the gun rules this land."

"Do you still think about her very much?"

"Yep. Guess I always will." He saw a shadow of hurt pass across her features, too, and he put a strong arm around her slim shoulders to reassure her. "Sometimes it seems like it was all foreordained, like some black cloud hangs over me. That's why I didn't want to get involved with you. Trouble just seems to follow me."

"Don't speak like that. Not on such a beautiful day. We can be happy, I know." She rolled over onto him, her wild black scented hair in his hands, her eyelashes brushing the vivid scar on his throat, and she began to kiss her lips down his bare chest, his abdomen . . .

170

The sound of the kitchen door banging, the clang of a bucket, made Juanita look up, surprised. It was the Opata woman bustling around. "Goodness! She must not find me here."

She slipped out of bed and pulled her lace-trimmed pantalets on, white against her amber body. "I'll get you some breakfast."

"It's you I'm hungry for."

He tried to hang onto her but she wriggled away, tapping him on the nose with a finger — "Later!" — and, her breasts bobbing, hanging onto her clothes, she started to the door, gave him a smile and quietly lifted the latch.

Pete got dressed and ambled along to the dining-room. When Juanita arrived she was bathed and perfumed, her hair brushed back, held by a scarlet ribbon, in gaucho pants of soft buckskin, and boots, her crisp starched shirt open at the neck. "Good morning, Mr Bowen," she said, as if greeting him for the first

171

time, and the Opata woman gave them an odd look.

"Hi," he said, helping himself to honeyed waffles and hominy grits. "Every time I see you, you look prettier than I remember."

"That's what love does to a girl," Juanita stage-whispered across the table as she poured coffee. "It's funny. I feel different. I'm not a virgin any more."

"Yeah?" He shook his head, his dark eyes troubled. "I shouldn't have. Makes me feel kinda guilty. You being so young."

"I'm seventeen. Plenty old enough. And it was I who seduced you, remember?"

Pete glanced at the fur rug before the hearth where they had romped. "I can't recall I resisted overmuch."

"I'll show you the range today. We can bring in some horses. We'll be needing a bigger remuda if Papa brings more men."

"Sounds fine," Pete watched the *señorita* as she animatedly talked. He liked her natural confidence in her beauty, her eyes glowing, her teeth sparkling white. And she knew plenty about running a ranch. "Any game about?"

"*Si*. Bring your rifle. We could do with some fresh meat."

★ ★ ★

They rode to the far corners of the Rioja range until they came to the red-mountain wall and timber climbing its sides. The girl had the true rider's seemingly effortless grace as her spirited black gelding swept her along before him, and his Arab-mustang thudded after her, snorting and prancing, skittishly, to show how much she was enjoying the race. At midday they stopped on the bank of the river and let the horses graze in a corner of lush grass.

Pete baited a line and threw it out and pretty soon he had four fine rainbow-hued trout glimmering on a stone. They lit a fire and roasted them in a mud casing. They flavoured them with sharp tangy lemon and wild thyme and chewed on fresh-baked bread. They washed the meal down with pure mountain water.

Juanita took off her stiff-brimmed Sevillean hat and lay back to doze in the sunshine, content to listen to the rushing babble of the water, which sounded like so many voices, ones she did not understand, possibly those of ancient Indian gods and spirits who protected this place.

Black Pete looked up at the endless blue sky. How peaceful it was here, far away from noisy towns and violent intruders. The only eyes watching were those of a golden eagle who lazily spiralled up high. It was hot in the sun and ideal for a siesta, but the attraction between them began to violently stir. The girl's shapely thigh against his made him rise on one elbow and toy with the buttons of her blouse, his fingers feeling for her breasts. She murmured, blissfully, and weaved her fingers into the thick hair on the nape of his neck to pull him into her.

"That was even better," she said afterwards, with a cheeky smile, as they slipped out of what clothing remained upon them and swam in the cool river. They clung to each other's bodies, slipping and sliding in the torrent, carried along, tumbling over smooth boulders, laughing and flicking the hair out of their eyes as they arrived in a natural pool.

Pete looked around sharply at the surrounding woods and hills. An apprehension in him. These days he did not like to be away too long from his guns. But everything seemed as quiet and peaceful as before. "We'd better think about gettin' back," he said. And they wandered along the bank back to their picnic spot, arm-in-arm, as naked as Adam and Eve before the fall.

What was that, though? As he dressed he noticed a movement in the pines. He reached for his rifle and kept low, indicating to Juanita to stay down. He sneaked behind a rock and squinted along his sights. A sturdy six-pronger buck stepped out onto a rock, his head held high, lord of his domain — until a rifle cracked out and the bullet caught him full through the side of his chest. He jumped, ran a few yards and collapsed, tumbling down the hillside.

"Good shot," Juanita said, for the buck was a good quarter of a mile away.

They rode over and Pete hefted the stag onto the back of his grey, tying it firm. They took it easy back, Pete singing a song about a Laredo cowboy, and Juanita joining in the choruses, and the sun was beginning to sink into a crimson bed of clouds as they reached the ranch-house, herding a group of half-wild mustangs before them. It was the first of several such idyllic days they spent together.

Sometimes, as they lay together on the fur rug before the mescal coals, they talked about maybe having a child, Pete helping her father run the ranch. Sometimes, it seemed to him that this sort of happiness could not last. And maybe to Juanita, too, for she clutched him as if needing to suck every moment of this joyous nectar . . .

15

EL CUCHILLO surveyed the remnants of his 'boys'. Four left, fortunately four of the best. There was Parson Gates, scarecrowish in his patched black coat, straw hair and battered hat. There was Shotgun Mason, one-time stage rider; a shooting incident meant he couldn't raise his right arm above his hip, which didn't prevent his accurate use of a double-barrel. There was the big man in the ragged dust-coat, Ephraim Jones, or Smith, or whatever name suited him. And there was a weathered range-hand, Charley Noone, long moustachios and in flapping leathers, who never left his rifle more than an arm's length away. All had this in common: they would not hesitate to kill.

"Now, you've shot poor ole Big Jake we definitely need some new boys."

"You told me to," Billy Joe protested.

"I just wanted to see," Lucifer grinned, "iffen you got the guts. Let's ride."

Billy Joe saddled his spotted Appaloosa with some difficulty, and struggled aboard with even more. "I'll call him Silver," he decided. He felt very high up, way above other mortals' heads. He clamped his derby tight, shook the reins, kicked his heels, but the Appaloosa didn't budge. "Hey ho, Silver," he shouted. No response.

"Ain't nobody nevuh showed you how to ride, son?" the livery agent asked. And gave the horse a whack over the rump with his broom. Silver plunged forward, running down the dusty main street, weaving from side to side as Billy Joe bumped helplessly up and down, trying, foolishly, to guide him loose-handed with the reins.

"Look at the kid go," Lucifer shouted, as they watched the Appaloosa roach his back, explode his heels, head down, bit between his teeth, putting two feet of air between the rider and saddle, and up again! "Yee-haaugh! Ride him, Billy Boy."

The advice was lost on the dentist, whose spine seemed to disintegrate at every bounce, until he finally went flying through the air and landed, every ounce of wind knocked out of him, on the extremely hard ground.

El Cuchillo led the horse back and said, "Git back on, boy. Watcha tryin' to do, ruin this horse? You cain't let him see he's beaten ya."

"Couldn't I catch the stage?" Billy Joe asked, lamely.

No, he had to pick himself up and try again. And this time he managed to hang onto the saddle-horn as they went trotting away. Oh, my God, he thought, at the prospect of many saddle-sore miles to go. And his spirits were not cheered by the sight of Miss Prissy, who came running out of the schoolhouse, followed by the children, catching up, and hanging onto his stirrup. "Don't go with these killers, Billy Joe," she cried. "Don't leave me. How long do you think you'll live?"

He stared ahead like a true steely-eyed Westerner, jogging after his friends, and she stumbled and fell in the dust. "Billy Joe," he heard her scream. "Forgive me."

What had he to forgive her for, he wondered. But what a spectacular descent he had made in so short a space of time! A few weeks before he had been the cossetted only son in his parents' comfortable home. Then he had been a foolish tenderfoot newly arrived in Diablo. And now look at him. He was the intimate of the roughest bandits in the Territory. He had broken the heart of a fine young woman. He had thumbed his nose at religion and goodness. And had killed his first man.

"Come on, Silver," he yelled, hanging onto the bouncing horse, trying to catch up with the others. "We're going to Silver City."

It was known as the toughest town north of the border.

★ ★ ★

They rode all day through the mountain and desert wasteland of southern Arizona. It was an area that had once been seabed. The tiny shells in the white sands testified to that. And in the distance they could see the mountains of New Mexico, rising like the bare bleak islands which once they had been.

For one so youthful Lucifer Grattan seemed to know every trail and landmark, and his keen eyes would decipher the tracks of kit-foxes, coyotes and sidewinders on the sand. He pointed out to Billy Joe the turkey vultures spiralling in the sky, no doubt keeping a beady eye on them, and humming-birds busy hovering in the cacti.

"We call it the Great American Desert," Billy Joe said, with awe. "But there's so much life."

"Yeah, it looks kinda dead around here, but there's a lot going on. The Apache can find drugs and food and water. They sure know how to survive."

"Or they did," Charley Noone put in, "before the white man came along. Let's hope we don't meet up with none of them boys."

"Aw, they're over in the high mountains of the Chiracahuas, ole Cochise and his nephew Geronimo," Shotgun said. "General Crook's got 'em on the run."

"So huccome they murdered a stageful of people outside Tucson two weeks ago?" Parson asked. "Carved up a Spanish lady, smashed her baby's head in on the rocks?"

"Yeah, before they would probably have taken the lady and kid captive. But now they massacre everybody they meet." And Charley looked around him fearfully. "They're fightin' to the death."

"Durn Injins," Ephraim said. "They're

like ghosts. Never know when those boys gonna appear."

They had this conversation as they squatted down in a dry wash at midday, and looked over their shoulders at the silent crags, uneasily.

At least, to Billy Joe the wash appeared to be dry, but Lucifer was digging down with a stick into the sand like some crazy dog. Not so crazy, though, for in a short while a small pool of water appeared, which their horses nuzzled at gratefully. The boys chewed on beef jerky, boiled up coffee, and smoked cigarettes for a while, before tightening their saddle cinches and going on their way.

That night El Cuchillo led them up a ravine until they reached a sheepherder's hut made of adobe — dried earth and straw plastered yearly so the rains wouldn't wash out the walls — it's pine beam ends holding ollas of water and strings of chilli peppers. The Mexican herder came to the door of his hut holding a shotgun, but when he saw six white boys armed to the teeth he put it aside and with ancient Spanish courtesy bade them enter his abode.

They cut the throat of one of his lambs and roasted it over his fire, while his wife and daughter, dark-haired and luminous-eyed in the flames, watched them from the shadows. They took his goatskin of *aguardiente* and pretty soon were shouting and laughing incoherently. Their bellies full, the boys decided to have a little fun with the women. Lucifer and Ephraim grabbed hold of the girl and dragged her into the back room. The *peon* pleaded with them that she was only fourteen and had never been dishonoured.

"Hell, it's time she was," El Cuchillo sniggered.

"Take me, *señor*," the mother begged. "Take me instead."

"Shee-it!" Charlie Noone cried. "If the fat squaw wants it she can have it as well." And pulling her down by the hair, he fell upon her and began burrowing at her clothing.

Billy Joe watched the wild orgy of drunken lust, his heart in his mouth. The Mexicans' terror seemed to enter his soul. Only Shotgun sat solemn-faced, smoking his pipe. He was an older man, his dark hair tinted with grey. He looked rather Mexican, himself. He glanced with disapproval as Parson unbuttoned to take his turn after Charley.

Finally the boys had had enough, and sprawled grunting and snoring on the bed on the softly-sobbing girl and her exhausted mother. Billy Joe was so stiff from the unaccustomed riding he stretched out on the dust floor and watched Shotgun tie the *peon* to a chair so he didn't cause any trouble in the night.

As they mounted up the next morning, El Cuchillo tossed a handful of silver dollars down at the feet of the herder. "Don't say we don't pay for our pleasures. If you speak of this to anyone we will come back and kill you. *Adios*."

186

He jerked his horse's head away and led them back down the ravine. "Don't worry," he grinned at Billy Joe. "I got plenty more dollars where they come from."

* * *

They made their way through a tangled mass of mountains in the foothills of which Silver City was nestled. They rode into town like a pack of wild dogs, alert, scenting prey. Silver had been mined there for decades but the seams were running out and many of the menfolk had turned to rustling and horse-thieving instead. Indeed, a herd of longhorns had been parked in the narrow main street between the decayed two-storey Spanish-style houses, blocked in at each end by covered wagons.

"Looks like we're in luck," El Cuchillo yelled, glancing at the brands. "I bet Sam Cook and his boys have been on a little moonlighting expedition along the Rio Grande. He'll be in the saloon arranging a price."

They pushed through the milling throng of beeves and found Cook, a thin-faced man in a tall Stetson, auctioning the stolen herd. Lucifer called for two bottles of Randall's rye whiskey and found a table. "Go over and tell him I want a word."

Billy Joe pulled back his suit coat to reveal the .38 stuck in his belt and strolled over to Cook. The cattle-thief ignored him at first, swatting him away as if he were a troublesome fly. When Billy Joe finally got his attention Cook's pale blue eyes seemed to look through him, as if he saw but didn't see. He slowly nodded, studying the youth, before returning to the bidding.

Whew, Billy Joe thought! Some creepy character! Cook's eyes had given the impression he was hollow inside. Will I become like that, he wondered? Is that what dispensing death does to you?

He tried to look tough, drinking the

whiskey by the neck when Cook joined them. "I got a job for you, Sam," El Cuchillo said. "Wanna hire twenty of your boys. Paying silver."

"What's the deal?"

"Won't take more than a day. Gonna wipe out a nest of greasers bin gittin' up my nose."

"Hey, mister, can I come?" A scrawny Irish kid of about twelve, Henry Antrim by name, had been hanging about them. His mother ran a boarding-house in town. "I can shoot."[1]

"Sure, when you're outa short pants," El Cuchillo laughed.

Suddenly Billy Joe was buffaloed by the potato lightning and hit the deck. The boys grinned and used him as a makeshift spittoon. Somehow he managed to reel outside to the urinal,

---

[1] Seven years later, under his new name of Billy the Kid, he would become the most famous outlaw in the world.

but the ground swung up and cracked his skull and pinned him there. He was unable to move as high-heel boots trod about, pissing over or on him. "How depraved can I get?" he wondered, as El Cuchillo hoisted him to his feet. "The lowest of the low."

"You can say that agin," Lucifer drawled, giving him a kick on his way. "Go find yourself some hole to sleep."

Billy Joe reached the main drag before he collapsed. He lay there all night, his head stuck out so that any passing wagon might have cracked his skull. The saint who protects drunkards preserved him from that.

When he woke in the morning he found his watch and wallet had been stolen. "Wouldn't be surprised if it wasn't that little runt Henry. Still, at least he didn't slit my throat," Billy Joe soliloquised. "This drinkin' ain't all it's cracked up to be. I'm gonna have to try to give it up. What would Prissy say if she saw me layin' here?"

He tried to air out in the sunshine his stained and stinking suit. He staggered back into the saloon where El Cuchillo was sitting in an all-night game of *chusas*. Billy Joe's guts churned painfully. His mouth was like the bottom of a bird-cage, as the saying goes. His head pounded. He was still on another plane. He needed another drink. He experienced the alcoholic's next torment. The booze was there under his nose. But he had no cash. And nobody would buy him one. He begged but they refused.

"We're moving out," El Cuchillo said. It was time to head back to Arizona.

★ ★ ★

Billy Joe bounced after the band of outlaws. "What have I gotten myself into? I haven't even cleaned my teeth," he moaned to himself.

It was exquisite relief when the hard men finally stopped riding that night and squatted down like a pack of wolves to devour an antelope they had shot. Billy Joe stood by the fire and thought he would practise spinning his revolver like El Cuchillo did. The .38 went off and nearly blew his foot apart.

"I haven't quite got the hang of that yet," he said apologetically.

"Where'd you find this fool," Cook snarled. "He's unbelievable."

"He ain't nuthin' to do with me," Lucifer replied, traitorously. "Jest some punk . . ."

"He's fit to have woke up every durn 'pache within twenty miles."

"Aw Gawd," Parson wailed, for that idea would put a shudder up any man's spine. "We'd better move on, boys."

"You sure got a lot to learn," El Cuchillo spat out as they hurriedly re-saddled their broncos. "We're right in the middle of Jicarilla territ'ry."

16

MIGUEL DEL RIOJA had not had a lot of success in recruiting men in Tucson. He had gone along to Munoz's corral to watch the breaking of mustangs. Most of the *vaqueros* there had shrugged, or shook their heads as they sat on the rails or leaned against the adobe walls. He only managed to recruit seven to his payroll and then by offering them exorbitant wages. It seemed word had filtered through of the pressure his *rancho* was being put under.

"You'd think it was the touch of death to work for me," he muttered to himself. And that summer it had been. He had lost count of how many of his men had been killed.

Nor did the Land Grants Commission office seem very impressed by the deeds, written on ancient parchment, he showed them. The matter would have to be looked into. But he had done as the *gringo* suggested, and announced his claims in the town newspaper.

The governor had been particularly unhelpful. He had kept Rioja waiting hours in his ante-room and had been brusque to the point of impoliteness. What could he do? Diablo City had elected its own sheriff, as was the case in these new settlements, hadn't it? Rioja would have to abide by the decision of the majority. "You have to bend with the wind," he said. "The old days are gone."

Angrily, the white-haired *haciendado* tossed a pouch of silver towards him. "Here! Will this help you bear my petition in mind? I am told this is the thing to do."

The governor gave an oily smile. "Tryin' to bribe a government official, huh?" He tucked the pouch into a drawer. "I'll have to see what I can do. This might buy you a morsel of protection."

Rioja stalked out of the governor's palace, angrily leaped onto his mustang and was about to lead his men out of town when he saw a troop of the 3rd Cavalry trailing into town with their pack-mules. They were dust-stained, weather-beaten, long-haired and unshaven, and had a disconsolate air. At their head was a queer-looking cove in a sun-helmet, white gauntlets and a canvas suit. He was tall and upright, straddling a mule, his fierce blue eyes and prow of a nose peering alertly through bushy mutton-chop whiskers.

He called his men to a halt, dismounted, and was about to enter the gates of the palace. Rioja doffed his sombrero and asked, "Aren't you General Crook?"

The tall man nodded at him. "I am."

He was about to pass when Rioja said, "Can I speak with you for a few moments, *señor*?"

"Is it important?"

"To me it is."

"We've been out for a month chasing Apache, futilely I might say, so make it snappy." The general beckoned Rioja to sit in the shade beside a trickling fountain in the courtyard. "Don't beat about the bush. Out with it, man."

"I am Miguel del Rioja. I own a *rancho* on the Diablo. I am being persecuted by a group of *renegados* based in Diablo City. In the past year they have been doing everything they can to run my people off. They have been stealing our cattle, burning our crops, attacking our men whenever they go into town or anywhere near. They have murdered a score of my *vaqueros* this summer. They are holding up our supply pack-trains. They have raped the womenfolk of sheepherders in the adjacent hills, tortured any who complain. They are led by one known as El Cuchillo, a youth who pretends to have authority to maintain law. Their only law is the law of Hell. They dry-gulched and killed my own son three weeks ago. They are cheats and backshooters."

"Yes, I heard you'd been having some trouble." General Crook reached out and patted the old *hidalgo*'s shoulder. "Bear up. I'm afraid you'll have to see this through yourself. The army can't interfere in civilian matters."

"They can't? Not even if the army itself is backing these *bandidos*?"

"What do you mean?"

"I mean that sappers from Fort Apache were involved only last week in trying to blow up our water supply, divert the course of the Diablo. It would have ruined me."

"Sappers? Be more explicit, sir."

"I mean army personnel, using army explosives and mules. We had to fight them off. Maybe you should check your stores."

Crook stroked his whiskers and frowned. "Maybe I should. But I am a busy man. My prerogative is to fight the Apache, defend lives in the Territory."

"Ach!" Rioja shrugged. "Don't our lives count? What else can I expect from Americanos?" He turned on his heel, climbed on his mustang, and led his men galloping away.

17

EL CUCHILLO and his gang of 'deputies' rode into Diablo City and lost no time tumbling into the Silver Nugget saloon to slake their thirsts. Billy Joe, somewhat saddle-sore, tied up his ornery Appaloosa and stepped after them along the wooden sidewalk. He was aware of folks eyeing him, men, even big ones, hastily stepping out of his way. Nobody had ever stepped out of his way like that before.

"I can blast the guts out of man or beast with one of these," Lucifer was saying as he stood in the centre of his cronies, holding his Magnum. "Blunt-nosed manstoppers. They tear the insides apart."

He raised the big gun, pointed at Billy Joe. There was the crash of an explosion, a smashing of bottles on a shelf, as, simultaneously, the boy's hat was whisked from his head. For a second Billy Joe froze, tempted to go for his gun. He stooped and picked up his shattered bowler. "Very funny," he said, as the men roared.

"Just remember your lil .38 ain't no match for this," El Cuchillo sneered.

Billy Joe looked into the mocking green weasel eyes in their slits. "How's your wound?" he asked. "You want me to clean it up?"

"Piss off, half-pint," El Cuchillo said, an evil snarl on his thin face. "I've sure had enough of you." And he turned his back to the boy, blocking him out.

"Can I get you a lemonade?" Fingal O'Rafferty smirked.

Lucifer half-looked back over his shoulder and made a limp-wristed gesture. "Why don't you give him a job with your powder-puff gals?"

Billy Joe's mouth went dry and his heart began to thud. Why were they talking to him like this? Why must he be held up to ridicule? Why couldn't he be accepted as one of them? He had killed, hadn't he? He watched the gang swagger over to the big table in the corner. Three Hispanic farmers and two tame Indians, probably Opatas or Yaquis, up with the bull-teams delivering supplies from Sonora, were already sat there.

El Cuchillo kicked a chair from under one of the Hispanics and growled, "Get outa here."

"Don't look so down in the mouth," Fingal said to Billy Joe, passing him the lemonade. "Drink this. It will do you more good than any whiskey. Be warned, young man, if you mix with curs one day they'll turn on you."

Billy Joe drank the tangy fresh lemon-juice. Yes, it was better than any whiskey. It made him feel clean. He nodded at Fingal to show he understood. The Indians and Hispanics had gone to sit at another table, but Lucifer was having fun snaking his sixteen-foot bullwhip out to crack over their heads. The Indians sat

201

sullenly staring into space, ignoring him, but the other three looked angry and resentful.

"Mister Grattan loves to play the big man. Some of us citizens are beginning to find him very tiresome," Fingal sighed. "He's driving my customers away."

"Yes, and his friends, too." Billy Joe remembered the awful night in the sheepherder's hut, the ordeal of terror the Mexican and his women had been put through. He was beginning to be sickened by his new companion's braggart ways. Why was he consorting with them? They were bullies, sadists, racists. He turned on his heel and walked out of the saloon, and across to his pawnbroker's shop.

"Well, he certainly made a mess of my hat," he muttered. "That's really going too far." He tossed the bowler away. It was time to get rid of that symbol of city life. He chose a wide-brimmed, low-crowned plainsman's hat from the shelf. He tried it on before a

202

mirror. Yes, that was better. He looked more the part. He had had enough of the gutter and its mire. He bathed and put on a rough broadcloth suit that somebody had pawned, selected a pair of hand-tooled boots. He tied a loose bow knot to the neck of a soft white shirt. He was a different man. A true westerner now.

He heard a clatter of gunshots and saw one of the Mexican farmers back-pedal out of the batwing doors of the saloon to land in the dust of the street. He was quickly followed by his four companions. Lucifer came out after them, lashing his bullwhip across their backs, around their legs and necks. They picked up the fallen man and staggered off down the street.

"Isn't it time somebody stood up for those people?" Billy Joe asked himself.

He locked up the shop and walked down towards the white Spanish mission church. The cross on it's bell-tower was dark against a blood-streaked sky as the day waned. A shiver passed through

Billy Joe. Maybe more than a shiver. He felt elated by the crimson sunset. Suddenly that simple cross took on significant meaning. He knew how St Paul had felt on the road to Damascus. He entered the church and made obeisance to the altar. A grey-haired priest was lighting candles. Billy Joe knelt before him. "Father," he said. "Will you hear my confession?" He wanted to cleanse himself.

It was dark when he left the church. He was going to take his Appaloosa to the livery when he saw El Cuchillo leave the Silver Nugget. Why did he have such a furtive air about him? He glanced back and forth along the main street as if to ascertain that he was not followed, and hurried off down a side alleyway. What's he up to, Billy Joe wondered.

There was only one way to find out. Billy Joe kept into the shadows and trailed the so-called sheriff along behind the ramshackle houses. Lucifer climbed up the hillside as if headed for the mines and suddenly stopped outside a small cabin. Billy Joe saw him knock, pause for a few moments and enter.

Maybe El Cuchillo had an assignation with some lover? Billy Joe shrugged. It was none of his business. He was about to return to his horse . . . but a strong prompting drew him to the cabin. So now he was a peeping-Tom? He tripped over some rocks in the darkness and held his breath, but nobody heard him. There was a faint glow in the cabin window. He crept up, tried to peer through. It was effectively curtained. He could hear the murmur of voices inside. He stepped round the back and put an eye to a crack in the logs, squinting through. He could see a man in dark broadcloth sat at a table. He was wearing a Quaker hat, and a white bandanna masked his face. On the other side of a flickering candle sat Lucifer. His pale face was tense and he looked kinda uncomfortable.

"A fine mess you made of it the last

time," the man was saying. "Serves me right for hiring boys instead of men."

"They ambushed us. They knew we were coming," Lucifer whined. "I didn't get this souvenir in my thigh for nothing. We hardly knew what hit us."

"How could they have known?"

"Well, it mighta been that fella calls hisself Missouri. Thought I saw him gunned down. But when I went back his body had gone."

The man was silent for moments while he considered this, and Billy Joe had a strange sensation of recognition, his build, his voice, somebody he had seen about the town. But he couldn't put a face to him and there were numerous businessmen wore dark frock-coated suits: the banker, the undertaker, the assayer. Yes, maybe it was the assayer? He would have an inside knowledge of mining. And the masked man was drawing a bag of silver from his coat pocket, passing it across to El Cuchillo.

"We've invested a lot of money in you, Grattan, and you've failed all the way along the line," the man said. "If anything goes wrong this time it could be your last pay-off. You understand what I mean?"

"I've got some good boys. We'll ride in and make mincemeat of them. Don't you worry."

"We want this settled," the muffled voice insisted. "You going to hit them tonight."

"The horses are tuckered out. We've had a long ride. And the boys are gittin' whiskeyed up. I'm swearin' 'em in as deputies and issuing 'em badges. We'll hit them tomorrow night. There'll be no mistake."

"There had better not be. We want them wiped out. All of them. Like a nest of rats."

"It'll be a pleasure, boss. The sooner we get our hands on that land the sooner we all get rich, eh?"

"You'll get your share."

Lucifer picked up the silver as he

got up to go to the door, and Billy Joe stepped back into the darkness. He watched him retrace his footsteps back to the town. As he did so the masked man emerged, climbed onto a horse, and rode off in another direction.

"He sure don't want anyone to know who he is," Billy Joe muttered as he watched him go.

18

WHY should he worry about some Mexicans? He had his dentist's business to mind. What had it to do with him? Let them fight their own battles. Thus Billy Joe berated himself as he hung onto the irksome Appaloosa, who never seemed to do as he was told. He had made his choice. He was a badman now. Why was he doing this? He would only end up in bigger trouble. But the vision of the cross against the blood-red sky the night before returned to him. Hadn't St Paul himself been a robber before he saw the light? The raping of those poor Mexican *peons*, the killings, the whippings had sickened him. He had to go.

He had told the boys he was going to get in some riding and shooting practice and they had laughed as he had galloped out of town towards Fort Apache. He had finally persuaded the headstrong Appaloosa to slow down, and had circled back around the town. He followed the river towards the Rioja range. The day was hot and he was sweating as he rode through a valley of green grama grass and huge pink rocks scattered as if by some giant's hand. Suddenly a bullet spanged into the dust before the horse's nose, making the Appaloosa rear and whinny and nearly unseat him. Billy Joe looked up and saw a Mexican with a rifle riding down towards him. Another shot cracked out from behind him, almost taking off his new hat. The boy spun the horse around and saw a second *vaquero* not far off. He reached for his Storekeeper — a small revolver against two rifles? He had no chance. The sweat went cold on his back and his mouth dried with fear as he realised they could easily kill him and probably would do. He slowly raised his hands.

The dark faces beneath sombreros

grinned as they drew near and both men spun their lariats to send them snaking out over Billy Joe's shoulders, jerking him to the ground. The boy got up, spitting dust, and found himself pinned tight by the lariats. "For goodness sake!" he said. "I've come to help you."

"How shall we keel heem?" one of the vaqueros asked.

"Slowly, I theenk. We caught ourselves a leetle peenk peeg."

"Don't be silly. *Donde este rancho Señor del Rioja??*" Billy Joe stuttered in basic Spanish. "*Mi amigo.*"

The two *charros* chattered to each other like shrill parrots until one grimaced. "Maybe we keel you later." He released the rope. "Come."

They rode like the wind beside him, yipping and yelping, as Billy Joe hung around the galloping Appaloosa's neck, and charged through the open gate of the ranch in a swirl of dust.

A lanky Americano was about to mount up beside a girl. "Howdy," he said, squinting up at the boy. "What brings you here?"

"Missouri! Aren't you? Lucifer said you were dead."

The girl laughed. "Well, you fooled one of them."

"Nope. I ain't no ghost," Pete grinned. "Waal — ?"

"I've come to warn you. Lucifer's enlisted another score of men. They're all hardened gunfighters. They're going to attack tonight."

"They are? That's real friendly of you to let us know. Ain't you Billy Joe, the idjit who was plannin' to get hitched?"

"Miss Prissy and I are temporarily estranged. This is serious, Missouri. Are these the only two men you've got? You can't hope to survive."

"Any idea of their plan?"

"El Cuchillo said we — I mean they — would come along the ridge, across the river there and scale the rancho walls."

Pete glanced at Juanita and back at

212

the boy. "We'll be ready for 'em. You had better water your horse, have a bite and get back."

As he sat in the kitchen and the Opata woman cooked him up some ham and eggs, Billy Joe asked, "Where's Señor Rioja?"

"He's away."

"How do we know," Juanita warned, "this boy hasn't come to spy out the land?"

"What shall we do? Lock him up?"

"I'll swear on the bible, if you got one?"

Juanita studied his eyes, tossed her black hair swinging back and smiled. "No, I reckon we trust you."

"How will you hold out?"

Black Pete spun the cylinder of his Frontier. "You know, old Sam Colt wasn't just a brilliant engineer and salesman of his product. He used to have an act demonstrating laughing-gas in his young days."

"He didn't?"

"Yep. He sailed round the world

before the mast. He was quite a character. He even whisked a friend condemned to death out of a New York jail right under the noses of the authorities. He invented a thing called submarine mines. He demonstrated them to the top brass out in Chesapeake Bay, I think it was. But they were too short-sighted to see their military worth."

"What has this got to do with us, Pete?" Juanita asked.

"When I was a kid and I heard about that experiment I decided to have a try myself in our river at Catfish Falls. It was what they call a qualified success. The local population didn't appreciate what I was doin' and I got a whuppin' for my pains."

"Yes?" she smiled, patiently, touching his hand. "Are you sure you haven't had too much sun?"

"Mebbe. But I fancy trying again. We got explosives, ain't we, what those sappers kindly gave us? And we got wire . . . "

"Pete," she yelled, and flung her arms around his neck, kissing him. "You're crazy, but I love you."

"Heck," he grinned. "That sure is nice to know. Billy Joe, you better be on your way. Juanita and me's got work to do. And if you ride with 'em make sure you stay back when they all head for the river."

* * *

A horned moon was half risen when the night-riders showed on the skyline and came charging down towards the river. "Now!" Juanita whispered as she knelt beside him on the ancient adobe wall of the rancho.

"Wait for it," Pete gritted out. "We ain't spent all afternoon layin' that wire for nuthin'. Let 'em get well and truly in there."

He watched nearly a score of men urging their horses down the steep bank, watched the beasts swimming the river which was deep and wide at this point. "Makes me feel like some admiral in command of some naval operation," he said, as he thrust down the plunger to detonate the explosives and saw spouts of water spiral into the night sky. There were shrill screams as limbs and heads were torn from bodies and rained down on the placid moonlit water. "Though I feel sorry for the poor dumb horses. They ain't done nuthin' to deserve gittin' blown to smithereens."

Half of the attackers had escaped and, struggling back onto their terrified beasts, were returning to the far bank to reform. Pete saw El Cuchillo in his black waistcoat and white shirt waving at them, urging them to try again at another spot along the bank. He was surrounded by his cohort of cronies, Charley, Shotgun and Ephraim, and in their cowardly way they stayed where they were as the men and horses plunged in. And well for them that they did. Pete pressed the plunger, more explosives went off, and the carnage was repeated. There were no survivors this time.

Black Pete reached for his rifle and took aim at the small group on the bank. But they were galloping away towards the woods and were swallowed up by the rocks and darkness as the shot cracked out.

"Damn," Pete hissed. "That boy's got snake eyes."

He sighted on another rider who broke from the bushes. He was on a spotted Appaloosa. He let him follow El Cuchillo.

"I think we're safe for a while more," he said, as he watched them go. "We better get them bodies outa there afore they pollute the water supply."

"I will help you."

"Nope. Go back to the house. This is gonna be grisly work."

"I am part of this," she said.

"Do what I tell you, gal."

She stood on tiptoes to kiss his hairy cheek. "Pete, thank you, once again, for saving my father's ranch. I'll go make a fire, have some coffee ready for when you're done."

She stood with an arm around his waist for moments and looked at the scene of desolation, hearing the whinnying scream of some injured horse. "Why must we be always at each other's throats? Why can't we humans live at peace in this fine land?" she whispered.

"I don't know. It's a question I've asked myself," he muttered. "Seems like man's a killin' animal and that's all there is to it. I sure never did believe in all that crap about the meek inheriting the earth. Those bloodthirsty varmints brought this on themselves. So I ain't gonna be buryin' 'em. The wolves can have a feed."

"Eugh!" — the girl shuddered and clung to him — "I suddenly feel as if a shadow has passed over my own grave, as if one of us will go."

"Come on," he said, gently, and jumped to the ground to help her down.

19

"HEY, girls and boys," Double-barrelled Annie squealed, as she peeped over the batwing doors. "The cavalry's arrived. It's gonna be a bumpy night."

"What on earth would you be talking about, girl?" Fingal asked, as he busied himself behind the bar.

"A whole durn platoon I tell you. Aw, shoot! He's sending 'em off. Jest some ole officer left behind. Looks like he's headin' in hyah." She quickly wobbled on dainty trotters to perch on a box by the bar and pouted her cupid lips into her most coy and seductive expression.

Lucifer Grattan was busy drowning his sorrows in a river of whiskey, the remnants of his gang and Billy Joe beside him, but he looked up, almost fearfully, as Major Absolom

Purdy stepped into the saloon in his high-knee'd boots, a feathered plume dangling from a visored shako. He was bow-legged but big-chested, his ruddy countenance and beaky nose giving him the air of a man who was accustomed to being obeyed.

"Good-evenin' to you, sorr," Fingal greeted him, accentuating his Irish burr. "What would be bringing you and your men to Diablo City?"

"Our horses would be bringing us man," the major replied, unable to restrain a slight smile at his wit as he removed his helmet, and brushed the dust from his dark-blue, double-breasted frock-coat, with its rows of gilt buttons and braid of rank on his sleeves. He adjusted the dragoon's sabre which hung tip-touching the floorboards. "All the way from Fort Apache. Just showing the flag, you know."

"Ah, you wouldn't be on what they call manoeuvres, then?"

"That is none of your business. But I can assure you I go where

I feel like going," the major said, as he removed his white gauntlets. "I've sent my platoon to make camp on the outskirts of town. They won't be getting any shore leave, so you needn't look so pleased with yourself. Got anything decent to drink?"

"For you, sorr, the best in the house. Iced Hailstorms. My own version of the south's mint julep." Fingal began preparing the cocktail. He had recognized the major as a turncoat who, after the war, had taken the oath of allegiance and accepted a commission with the North. He passed a brimming glass over and said, "There t'is now. Here's to the stars and stripes. What else can I be offering you?"

"One or two of my officers have mentioned that you provide more sophisticated — ah — entertainers than is customarily available." He glanced along at Double-barrelled Annie, but quickly looked away as she simpered and twiddled her fingers at him.

"Your officers tell you right, major.

221

But you're looking in the wrong direction. Now Esmeralda over there, she's an expert in titillation."

The lithe negress in her tight dress and purple boa gave him a wide grin and a wave. "Wha, I do declare we got a real live Une-yun general in our midst. Don't you love that vulture feather in his hat? Who's gonna be the lucky lady tonight?"~

"Major," the major corrected, as he nodded at her. "I must say she looks a little more stylish than the other sluts about these parts."

"Would Esmeralda be taking your fancy?" Fingal murmured, with a wink, leaning over the bar. "I keep a cabin at the back specially for private parties for respectable gentry, the married kind, you know."

"Yes, I've heard. I must have privacy. I'm expecting a gentleman friend to join me. How much?"

"Inclusive rates, dinner, wine, and Esmeralda? Let's see, that would only set you back twenty dollars."

"Twenty dollars!" The major snapped his high-browed if balding head back, and his sword rattled alarmingly. "The going rate for whores is usually a dollar, two at the most, especially a nigger gal. Why, before the war they considered it an honour to be serviced by a white gentleman."

"Yes, but the finest food. Steaks, ortolans, meringues. And finest French wines," Fingal lied, for it was the dago red he had diluted. "Would you care to order now?"

"You're a bit pricey, but what the hell," the major said. "Yes, send Esmeralda in, if she's the best you've got. She reminds me of a slave we once had on our plantation."

"Ah," Fingal sighed. "The good old days before we had to set them all free. A terrible blow to the southern culture."

Major Purdy sipped at his Hailstorm and raised a candle to light a cigar, looking around through the flickering shadows at the few slouched and slovenly men frequenting the place at this late hour. "Tell me, are you familiar with a young man known as El Cuchillo?"

"The very man. He's standing right there. Poor boy's had a terrible shock. He's a bit pixillated. Most of his men have been massacred. His pal Parson Gates among them."

"Massacred? By God! Tell him I want a word."

"Remember, major. Be firm. You're dealing with riff-raff."

"Send him over." The major stomped over to a darkened corner where he could not be overheard. Lucifer looked alarmed when Fingal told him to get over there. "What's he want with me?" he said.

"That's what I'd like to know," Fingal muttered to Billy Joe.

El Cuchillo stumbled drunkenly over to the military man, and Billy Joe watched him waving his arms, going "Boom! Boom!" He's telling him about the mines, he thought.

"Massacred," the major thundered, as he returned to the bar. "On a peaceful mission. This is something we're going to have to look into. We can't have Mexicans shooting at our upholders of law. Practically the whole posse wiped out."

"That's right," El Cuchillo nodded.

"Sure, a posse of brigands," Fingal put in. "Your gentleman friend, major? I presume he doesn't wish to be seen? He knows the way around the back, does he? There's a red light above the door."

20

BILLY JOE watched from the shadows at the back of the saloon. Somebody was approaching the cabin door beneath its red lamp. Who was this? A man in a black Quaker hat, a high-collared caped coat and a white scarf that effectively masked his face. Surely it was the man he had seen in the other cabin giving El Cuchillo his orders? Yes, there was something tantalizingly familiar about him. The man glanced around, tapped on the door, and went inside. Billy Joe would have given anything to take a peep, but there were no chinks in these walls. The cabin was solidly built and the windows masked with red damask. He saw Fingal take in trays of food and bottles of liquor. He saw Esmeralda go in, giving a shrill giggle. Then Major Purdy was at the lighted doorway shouting that they did not wish to be disturbed. And the door slammed shut.

How to get in there? A crazy idea occurred to him, taking his breath away by its effrontery. Did he dare? Yes, he had to see that man's face. He nipped into the saloon by the back door. He could hear Fingal busy at the bar. He went along a corridor and into a changing-room used by the dancing-girls. There were dresses and wigs hanging from hooks on the walls. Billy Joe pulled his shirt and boots off and rolled his trousers up. What would suit him? Possibly this virginal white satin thing? He slipped the frock over his head, pulled a blonde wig on, powdered and painted his face, surprised by the apparition in the glass. A different person. A fallen dove! He squeezed his toes into a pair of high-heel slippers and tottered out.

At his knock on the cabin door Major Purdy presented himself. "Yes?"

"I'm the new girl. Fingal sent me."

"Come in, my dear," the major boomed in his manly way, drawing *her* into the well-appointed cabin. There was a table lit by candles and littered with empty plates. Sat back in the shadows on an armchair was the man in the black suit. He still had his hat on and had drawn the white scarf over his face at Billy Joe's entrance. There was a large gilt-edged mirror on one wall, and other knick-knacks around a roaring fire. The major led the pert-nosed *blonde* over to a comfortable, crimson-covered horsehair sofa. "My, what a little charmer. What can I get you to drink?"

"Make it a whiskey and soda," Billy Joe said, trying to pitch his voice high and fluttering his eyelashes. "My name's Susie. I'm new arrived in town."

"Ah sho wondered where yo' come from," Esmeralda drawled as she sprawled in her silver dress on a cushion-covered divan.

"Fingal thought I'd better get acquainted."

"You girls certainly get around," the major laughed, unbuckling his sword. He poured them drinks and sat down beside *Susie*, putting a clumsy arm around her. "Well, sir, as I was saying, your El Cuchillo seems to have made a fine mess of things yet again. I paid out good silver for those twenty dead gunmen."

"El Cuchillo's not all to blame" — the stranger's voice was muffled by the scarf — "Rioja's got some mystery mercenary working for him. My spies tell me Rioja was seen returning this morning from Tucson with reinforcements. All I want to know is what are we going to do about him?"

"Don't worry about it" — the major's fingers were playing with the necklace around *Susie*'s slim neck — "I'm going to take my platoon and blast hell out of 'em tomorrow. We won't be taking any prisoners. We'll see who can play with explosives. And then we'll carve that land up between you and me."

"Careful what you say, major," the muffled voice said.

Major Purdy was already well-intoxicated on Fingal's Hailstorms and 'French wine', and replied airily, "Oh, relax, man. These are only a couple of drunken doxies. They haven't a clue what we're talking about."

"What a mighty Excalibur," Esmeralda shrilled unsheathing the sword and whirling it above her head, dancing about like a dervish, and collapsing in a heap of laughter on top of the major. "We're professional ladies, eh, Susie? Even if we did know what you boys was gassin' 'bout we sworn to secrecy."

Billy Joe took the opportunity to wriggle out of the major's embraces. "That's true." Swishing in satin and lace he went over to slip onto the masked man's knee. "Don't be shy, honey," he said, as he looked into fanatical green eyes.

"Sure, go on," Major Purdy urged. "You have Susie. Later we'll swap over."

"I'm not interested in sluts," the masked man said, trying to push Billy Joe away.

"I'm no slut," the youth replied, rolling his kohl-outlined eyes as he had seen girls do to impart an air of innocence. And he whipped the white scarf from the man's face. "Let's take a look at you, darling."

He was so shocked by the face he saw, however, that he could not help gasping out, "Reverend!"

"How the hell do you know me, girl?"

"I think I'd better be going," Billy Joe said, trying to escape, but Ebediah Spank's strong arms were hanging onto him now, his green eyes registering alarm.

"Or *are* you a girl?" Spank asked, pulling the wig from the youth's head. "Billy Joe! So this is what you do in your spare time?"

"You know that gal?" Major Purdy bristled. "I mean boy."

"Yes, we've met before, haven't we, Billy? Don't be silly, my little one," Spank twisted one of the boy's arms behind him. "You're not going anywhere. I'm going to have some fun with you."

"You mean he's a molly boy?" the major asked.

"I mean we're in trouble, major. This boy would give us away. In fact, I do believe he's spying on me."

Billy Joe tried to make a grab for his .38 Storekeeper tucked in his trousers beneath his skirts, but as he struggled and fumbled Major Purdy had his sword point at his throat. "Not so fast, young man, or lady."

"Yes." The Reverend Spank gave a broad-toothed grin and a horsey snigger. "I've been wanting to get my hands on you for some time. And you won't be seeing Miss Prissy afterwards. You won't be seeing anybody."

"No," the major said. "El Cuchillo

can cut his throat in the morning. Pity, really. A pretty little thing."

"You pervert!" Billy Joe smashed his bony fist into the reverend's nose. He saw the skin burst like a squashed tomato. But, after that, everything went black and he didn't remember any more.

21

BILLY JOE woke to see Esmeralda's delineated features as she leaned over him. She smacked him gently, but insistently, across his face. He was bound hand and foot and lying inside the cabin where he had first seen the masked man. A hurricane lamp gave a glow to the negress's dark-brown eyes, but instead of their customary mockery there was concern. "Ah surely thought they'd kilt ya. That reverend man hit ya on the head wid ya own .38."

"What happened?" the boy asked, touching his raw scalp with dread, as Esmeralda cut his ropes.

"Wha', don'cha 'member? Ya fought like a tiger to stop thet nasty ole man from gittin' his way. You still a virgin, honey chile!"

"That's a relief to know."

"You gotta git outa here. El Cuchillo's

got orders to slit your throat. So git on your hoss, boy, and git outa this town and keep goin'. Here, I brought ya your shirt and boots. I'll have my frock back, if you don't mind."

Billy Joe pulled off the dress, his mind in a whirl. "I've got to warn them, Esmeralda, or they'll be wiped out. I like Missouri, and his gal."

"Too late for that, Billy Joe. It nearly dawn and Major Purdy and his cavalry march out ten minutes ago. I just wait to see the coast clear."

"I've got to do something. It's not fair."

"Wha' kin a boy like you do? Leave well alone, Billy Joe. You git caught you know nuthin' 'bout me helpin' ya, is that clear?"

"Of course, and thank you, Esmeralda. You're a sport."

"Lawdy, thet's the first time I bin called dat! I brought your old hoss along. Ride, Billy Joe. Ride for your life. Those old boys dey got dis town tied up. There ain' nuthin' we kin do."

Billy Joe swung onto Silver and kicked him away at a gallop, thundering through the town's deserted main street, hanging low over his neck and pulling him round onto the trail for Fort Apache. It was a long way away, but it was the only hope . . . he had to try to get help . . .

22

MAJOR PURDY'S platoon had been warned about the possibility of mines in the river so they crossed the Diablo well before they reached the Rioja ranch and approached the gates with their holsters unbuttoned and their carbines at the ready.

Aroused by the clanging of the lookout's bell Black Pete ran out and leaped up beside the guard on top of the wall, warning him not to open up. "Let's hear what these varmints want," he snarled.

Miguel del Rioja and Juanita climbed up beside him and the *haciendado* called out to Major Purdy, who had drawn his column to a halt ten feet from the gates, "How can I help you soldiers?"

"Open up," the major shouted. "We

are a mission from Fort Apache."

Pete gripped the rancher's arm. "Hold on. I got a queasy feeling inside me this is some sort of trick. An' when I get that feelin' I ain't often wrong."

"I am sorry, *señor*," the rancher shouted down. "I cannot do that. This is private land. We not open our door to anyone. We have had too much trouble here. You may state your business from where you are."

"Why you insolent foreigner," Purdy blustered. "Would you defy the US Army? I'll have you all clapped in irons. I am here to arrest you for the cold-blooded murder of peace-officers. Open up, I say."

"They were no peace-officers. They were *bandidos*," Rioja called. "I would advise you and your men to withdraw, or you will get the same reception. We gave your sappers a taste of what to expect. We have been patient so far."

Purdy had half turned in his saddle and was saying something to one of his men, who had drawn something from his saddlebag and was striking a match.

"Hey, he's got dynamite!" — Pete raised his revolver and fired, his bullet cutting the fine horsehair pendant from the major's shako, making Purdy duck and turn his horse with alarm. But it was too late. The dynamite was thrown as the Union soldiers wheeled their horses away at the gallop.

"Get down!" Pete shouted, and threw himself upon Juanita, pinning her against the wall as the gate was blown in. Through the debris and dust he saw that one of their new *vaqueros* was lying dead. "Take up your positions on the wall. Shoot to kill."

"If we kill US soldiers they will hound us to death."

"We have no choice," Pete said, his face grim as he fed a bullet into the breech of the Spencer. "If we surrender peaceable that pompous devil will order us all shot, I'm sure of that."

"Surely he will let my daughter ride

out before we start killing each other?"

Pete anxiously met the girl's startled eyes. "I dunno. I wish now I'd done what you asked. Hogtied her and taken her back to Old Mexico."

"I'm not going. They would hold me hostage, threaten to kill me to make you surrender. Don't you see, father? I can't go."

Rioja reached out and squeezed her hand. "Go to your bedroom, lock yourself in and stay there until this is all over."

"I will go get my rifle. I am fighting alongside of you."

"Here they come," Pete gritted out, as he heard the bugler sound the order to charge. "I don't see how we can stop 'em, but we sure can try."

Riding two-abreast, the column of 'blue-bellies' came charging towards them, whooping like Indians, aimed at the breached gate of the ranch. "Fire!" Pete shouted, as he squinted along his sights and took out one of the leading horses, making others come

240

crashing and tumbling down upon it in whinnies of terror, rolling and crushing and breaking limbs.

Others swerved around the fallen ones and charged on, kicking up a cloud of red dust, the soldiers firing their carbines at the *vaqueros* lining the walls. Two more animals tumbled and ploughed head first, kicking their legs, but unable to rise again. Several soldiers were pitched from their saddles by the Mexicans' fusillade of lead.

Major Purdy raised his arm twenty paces from the gate, signalling his men to wheel away, but three of them ignored, or did not see, the signal and came on, hurtling through the gateway. They plunged their horses hither and thither in the forecourt of the ranch-house, firing revolvers wildly, until they were cut to pieces.

Two of the *vaqueros* had been killed by the soldiers' fire, and one was badly injured in the chest.

"They coulda had us that time if that officer had kept on comin'," Pete muttered, as he reloaded. "He was too keen on saving his own cowardly soul."

"It is not my life I am worried about," the rancher said, as he watched his daughter giving water to the injured man. "It is Juanita's."

"Me, too," Pete agreed, and it was true, for the threat of imminent death had been with him for so many years, fighting Northerners, outlaws, Comancheros and Comanches, it was a familiar companion. "But all we can do, *amigo*, is pray. We ain't got a hope in hell of holding out against these boys. An' I don't like the look of what they're up to now."

Two of the soldiers had charged up, getting down from their horses, lifting something heavy with them, to take up a position behind a fallen mount.

"They got a durn Gatlin' gun. And they're well within range. Keep your heads down, *muchachos*. Guess we're lucky it ain't a howitzer."

The Gatling began stuttering out,

spraying the adobe walls with its lethal message as one soldier cranked the handle and the other fed the belt through. A *vaquero* screamed as he foolhardily revealed himself and his head was half sliced off by bullets.

Pete waited until the leaden spray had passed before attempting to put the gunners out of action, but they were well concealed by the big cavalry horse. And here came another attack, this time the soldiers charging in two diagonal angles at them, shouting murderously to buoy up their courage. The Gatling gun stopped to allow the soldiers to pass, so the *vaqueros* could stand and return rapid fire.

"Got one!" Rioja shouted triumphantly, as a cavalry corporal was tipped from his saddle and was dragged bouncing away, his boot caught in his stirrup. In spite of the fact that they were facing almost certain extinction, his face was flushed by the excitement of battle. Pete glanced along and saw that Juanita, too, had a glint of determination in her violet eyes as she pulled her rifle tight to her shoulder and blazed away like a fury.

The rain of fire was too much for the cavalry boys who turned away and circled back to rejoin the watching Major Purdy. The machine-gun began rattling again, and Pete ducked down to peer through the haze of dust and gunsmoke to count how many were left of them. Seven *vaqueros* gone already. For the first time he considered surrendering, but, as he met Juanita's eyes, it was as if she had read his mind for she shook her head determinedly. "Never," she said.

"What are they doing now?" Rioja asked.

Through a hole in the battlements Pete saw that the two columns of cavalry were galloping away on either side of the *rancho*, encircling the walls.

"Looks like they're gonna try and breach the walls down at the far end," he said. "While them gunners keep us busy up at the front."

He could see Purdy sitting his horse nearly half a mile away, watching events through his telescope, directing them from a safe distance. Glancing across the river he also saw a small group of men in civilian clothes watching from the hillside. One was in a black suit and hat, a white silk scarf around his throat. The others he recognised as El Cuchillo, Charley Noone, Shotgun and the big man, Ephraim, in his duster coat.

"Hail," he muttered. "They're like damn coyotes waiting for us to fall."

Another faint sound came to his ears, a distant bugle. It wasn't Purdy's bugler. Looking along the valley Pete saw a plume of red dust and he could hear the drumming of hooves, and pretty soon he made out the pennants of the 3rd Cavalry, the sun flashing on sabres and visors and epaulettes, a cavalry column galloping towards them at a hell of a lick.

"It's a whole durn company," he said.

"Reinforcements," Rioja whispered, crossing himself. "There is no way we can hold them all off. Juanita, I order you to go to your room."

"Hang on," Pete said. "What 'n hell's happening? Who's thet feller on a mule? Ain't thet young Billy Joe by his side?"

"That's General Crook," Rioja cried. "I would recognize those mutton-chop whiskers anywhere. Can he be supporting these villains?"

"Nope. He's calling them off. Listen to that bugle-call." Pete got to his feet, the girl beside him, to stand on the parapet and watch the new cavalry arrivals rounding up Major Purdy's platoon. They were escorting them back to the main body, the machine-gunners along with them.

★ ★ ★

It was indeed General Crook. He had been investigating affairs at Fort Apache and enquiring about the whereabouts of the major, and why he was not where he ought to be. He had been marching to seek him out at Diablo City when he had come face to face with Billy Joe a few miles from the town. The youth had blurted out all he had heard of Purdy and Spank's plan to drive Rioja from his ranch and split the land between them.

"Are you prepared to give evidence on oath to that effect?" General Crook had demanded.

"I am, sir."

"Then come on, boy. Let's hope to God we get there in time."

Now the general was face to face with Purdy. "Hand over your revolver and your sword, sir," he roared at him, with righteous indignation. "You are a disgrace to your uniform and my regiment. See those bodies of good men lying there. Their blood is on your head. And that of many other peaceful cow-herders, too, from what I hear. Yes, you, sir. Don't give me that bluster. You are under arrest."

★ ★ ★

"Jesu, Maria," Juanita breathed. "I have heard this general is a just man. I believe our war is over."

The girl slipped an arm around Pete's waist as they stood on the rampart and watched Purdy reluctantly handing over his sabre. Suddenly she gave a gasp and stumbled, hanging onto Pete as the crack of a rifle shot sounded from the hillside.

Pete hung onto her, looking across the river, and saw the man in black sheathing a rifle as he turned his horse to ride away, quickly followed by his companions.

He turned his attention back to the girl, holding her in his arms, as her beautiful upturned face took on a distraught look. "Pete," she whispered. "Oh, Pete — "

They were the last words she spoke. A trickle of blood spurted from her lips. Her vivid violet eyes suddenly lost their light. And her dark-haired head fell to one side like a broken doll's.

"Juanita! No!" Pete stared at the girl, unbelieving. How could they? He carefully laid her down on the rampart and took her hands in his, gentle, delicate hands. But it was no good. She was lifeless.

Bowen's blood seemed to go cold as he knelt over her. It was as if part of him had died that moment with her. A huge emptiness entered his soul. He was frozen, unable to speak, like a statue.

"Oh, my God! Why have you deserted me?" Miguel del Rioja screamed with shock and anger. "First my beloved son. Now my daughter. Why her? Why my poor girl?" And he began sobbing forlornly as he knelt beside them, tears streaming from his eyes. "Why couldn't he take me?"

Pete Bowen gently closed the girl's eyes. He gripped the man's shoulder, and stood. His grief had been replaced by a cold rage boiling inside him.

"She will be avenged," he whispered. "I swear to you."

Like some automaton he descended the steps from the ramparts, calmly and methodically checked his revolvers, saddled his grey, and hoisted himself into the saddle. Straight-backed, he rode out of the shattered gates, remote and cold, as if his mind was on another plane. He jogged up to General Crook, who was standing in his solar topee and canvas suit, waggling a finger at Major Purdy. They turned as if they expected the horseman in his tattered mackinaw to speak to them. Pete pulled his Colt *Frontier* in his right hand and aimed it at the major's blue-covered chest. He fired point-blank. The major went spinning back, a hole blasted in his heart.

"See you in hell," Pete snarled.

Such was their surprise, before any of the soldiers could intervene Pete had put spurs to his Arab mustang, who sprinted away along the rocky valley. He was almost at the river when a sergeant aimed his rifle at his back. As he was about to squeeze the trigger General Crook knocked his arm up. "Don't shoot," he shouted. "Let him go."

He looked down at Purdy's bloody body. "Vengeance is mine, sayeth the Lord. There goes the Lord's executioner. We will catch up with him soon enough. At least he has saved us the bother of a court-martial for this villain."

Billy Joe ran and vaulted onto his Appaloosa, whipping it away to go galloping after Black Pete. They watched him go splashing across the river. "It looks like our young friend is intent upon doing the Lord's work, too," the general said, with a wry smile.

23

"WE'RE being followed," Lucifer Grattan shouted, as they hauled in their sweating horses on a ridge outside Diablo City. "It's that stranger and Billy Joe."

"One man and a boy," the bloody-nosed preacher jeered. "You can take them, can't you? Don't foul up this time. I've got to get back."

The preacher picked his way carefully around the back of the town to his presbytery as El Cuchillo and his men rode into the main street.

"Charley, you're the best shot with a rifle. Get up in the livery loft. Ephraim, hide out in the gunsmith's. Shotgun, you can side me. Make sure of the boy. The rest of us will concentrate on Missouri. OK?"

Lucifer jumped up onto the wooden sidewalk and went into the saloon with

Shotgun. Fingal did not speak as he poured them shots of whiskey. Early morning and the Silver Nugget was practically empty for it was a Sunday. El Cuchillo spun the cylinder of his Magnum, and licked spittle from his lips, nervously.

Black Pete dismounted on the edge of town and went forward on foot, his eyes alert for any ambush. It was deathly quiet except for the bell of the white-painted Presbyterian church that had begun to dolefully toll. Billy Joe edged along the side of the street. He could sense a tension in the town as if eyes behind curtained windows were watching them.

Outside the Silver Nugget Black Pete paused and eyed the sweated-up horses hitched to the rail. The silver-engraved butts of his Frontiers hung loosely forward on his hips and his hands were poised. "Lucifer Grattan," he shouted. "Come out of there. Or I'm coming in to get you."

Keep your eyes on the livery, Billy Joe

thought. That's what Pete had told him. He backed along the sidewalk towards the saloon batwing doors. But it was the gunsmith window that smashed and Ephraim appeared, his revolver blazing. Billy Joe raised Pete's Spencer and — 'Kee-oww!' — the big .52 slug cut Ephraim's eyes out. His lifeless body toppled out into a horse-trough.

'BLAM!' — a shotgun roared above his head and he saw Black Pete go down, his leg shot from under him.

Simultaneously, a bullet splintered the wall by his head and Billy Joe looked up to see Charley Noone kneeling in the loft doorway. He fed a slug into the Spencer and fired, carefully. And surely. Charley jerked in a death spasm as he collapsed, pitching forward to thud down into the dust.

Lucifer burst from the saloon doors, bending low, his Magnum belching flame and lead. He was in too much of a panic to aim carefully.

Although disabled, Pete had his Frontier in his hand and aimed up at the bedroom window of the saloon where Shotgun was manoeuvring to release his second barrel. The ageing Hispanic screamed as Pete's bullet took off the top of his scalp.

Billy Joe threw the Spencer away and pulled the .38 Storekeeper from his belt. "Lucifer!" he shouted.

Grattan spun on his boot-heels to face him, his long face white with fear. For seconds his green eyes glimmered, satanically, as they made contact with the youth's. "Billy boy." His thin lips flickered in a faint smile as he jerked the Magnum up and a manstopper crashed out. But he was a split second too late. Billy Joe's bullet cut through his aorta, blood spurted, and he was cut down like a sapling. He lay on the sidewalk coughing his last.

Billy Joe looked around him, his Storekeeper ready as the black smoke drifted, a smell of cordite, sweat, death and dust in his nostrils. But there were only a few curious townspeople peering like animals might, startled, and going back to whatever they were doing, simply glad it was not their turn this time. Gunfire was a common sound in that town.

"Hey, *amigo*, you did well," Pete shouted, huskily. "Help me up, will you?"

He examined the bloodstained jeans of his thigh, and winced. "A couple of inches higher and that would have bin the end of my marital prospects. Good job I had you around. Where did that other skunk git to? I've a score to settle with him."

"He may be in the church," Billy Joe said, helping Pete up to balance on his shoulder, and hobble away along the street.

A harmonium was playing loudly as Billy Joe kicked in the door of the church and Miss Prissy, standing in the choir-stalls to lead the singing, screamed to see him and the tattered bloody bearded stranger standing there. "Billy! What are you doing?"

"We want that mealy-mouthed

hypocritical friend of yourn," Billy Joe said. "He's the cause of all the trouble there's been."

The Rev Ebediah Spank, in his black suit, stood tall in the pulpit. "How dare you enter the house of God with those guns?" he shouted. "Begone! We are respectable folk here."

"You devil's spawn," Black Pete said. "You jest step outside. We gonna hang you for the murder of Juanita del Rioja."

"Pay no heed to them, my friends," the Rev Spank shouted, his bloodily split nostrils flaring, his eyes opening maniacally wide. "We are people of peace here."

He opened his big bible and from its hollowed-out interior produced a revolver — 'CRASH!' — he aimed it over the heads of the congregation at the tall 'prairie rat'. Pete, unflinching, extended his left arm and blew the preacher to pieces — three successive bullets — through his lungs, throat and nose. The preacher hung to the pulpit, his pale eyes bulging, his shattered face and body frothing blood, before he tumbled to the floor beneath the cross of his God.

"That's settled his hash," Pete muttered. "The murderin' bastard."

Holding onto Billy Joe's shoulder he limped back to the saloon as General Crook's cavalry column cantered into town.

"Ain't you gonna arrest these gunmen?" a miner asked the general as the undertaker busied himself with a tape-measure about the bodies in the dust.

"You can do as you like with me," Pete said. "But it seems to me you would be doing the right thing iffen you folks pinned a proper lawman's badge on this boy, Billy Joe. Then maybe you could git a little peace and order around here."

"That seems a good idea," the general put in, as he sat his mule. "It's high time you civilians looked after yourselves. The army hasn't got time to police your squabbles. We've got a war to fight. We will, of course, be conducting an enquiry into what has gone on here. Meanwhile, I agree you should elect this young man as your sheriff."

"All those in favour raise their hands," Pete told the crowd. "Right, that's settled. As long as you're agreeable, Billy Joe?"

"Well, yes, I guess so. I can be dentist, pawnbroker, and sheriff, too." Billy Joe beamed as Miss Prissy ran up to hang onto his arm, while Esmeralda snuggled up the other side of him, and an itinerant photographer moved in to record the occasion. "Gee, won't my mother and dad be surprised."

24

"I GUESS I'll be moseying on," Pete said, a couple of weeks later. "Billy Joe tells me two Texas Rangers have been in town asking about me. He directed 'em on along to Tombstone. Reckon I'd better head north."

"What am I going to do now?" Miguel del Rioja shook his white mane. He was still in a state of shock. "I am a lost man. I have nothing. Both my children gone."

"You've got your homestead," Pete said. "You've got a duty to make it prosper. That's what Juanita would have wanted."

Miguel looked up at the tall, limping man as he packed his Spencer in the saddle-holster and jerked the saddle cinches tight. "This land means nothing to me now without them."

Pete glowered at him. "Don't be a fool. Land is worth fighting for. Like Juanita fought. Pull yourself together, Miguel. You are only middle-aged — what, forty-five or so? You can father more children. Why don't you marry the Opata woman. She likes you, I know."

Miguel looked at the Indian widow-woman standing in her pinafore by the kitchen door watching them, her two toddlers by her side. And his eyes glimmered with hope and life. "Maybe you're right," he said.

Pete rode out of the shattered gateway and when he turned to wave he saw that Miguel was standing with his arms around the Opata woman and her children. He paused at the fresh-dug grave of Juanita, beside those of her mother and brother. He made a brief sign of the cross from forehead to heart, the way the Spanish people did, and nudged his mustang forward, riding out, biting back the tears in his eyes.

As he loped past Diablo City, in his

261

tattered mackinaw and flat-topped hat,
Billy Joe came riding out to greet him.
"Hi!" he called. "I wish I was coming
with you. But I'm getting married to
Miss Prissy tomorrow."

"Take care," Pete grinned at him.
"Don't do nuthin' I wouldn't do."

And without looking back he cantered
away along the Santa Fe trail.

"I sure won't," Billy Joe whispered to
himself as he watched the stranger go.

THE END

FIGHTING RAMROD
Charles N. Heckelmann

Most men would have cut their losses, but Frazer counted the bullets in his guns and said he'd soak the range in blood before he'd give up another inch of what was his.

LONE GUN
Eric Allen

Smoke Blackbird had been away too long. The Lequires had seized the Blackbird farm, forcing the Indians and settlers off, and no one seemed willing to fight! He had to fight alone.

THE THIRD RIDER
Barry Cord

Mel Rawlins wasn't going to let anything stand in his way. His father was murdered, his two brothers gone. Now Mel rode for vengeance.